"Mind if I flake out on that bed?"

Yawning broadly, Ken didn't wait for a reply. Without even removing his jacket, he slumped onto the coverlet, eyes closed.

"You're obviously in no shape to do anything else on that bed," Adrienne muttered to herself as she helped him undress. As efficiently as possible she removed everything—everything but his briefs.

Toward the end, she had to call upon the combined powers of the ancient gods to resist caressing his muscled shoulders, his powerful chest, his flat stomach....

She started guiltily when he opened one eye and mumbled, "I always sleep in the nude."

"Oh. Well, then...." Gingerly she began to remedy the situation—only to discover he was not as tired as he seemed....

THE AUTHOR

Regan Forest spent many exciting years overseas, but she has finally settled down to do what she's always wanted. Surrounded by her three children, her dogs and the Arizona desert, Regan is writing stories of adventure and romance.

Inspired by a true story, *The Answering Tide* is Regan's first Harlequin Temptation. With one Harlequin Intrigue already published and a second Temptation to be released later this year, Regan Forest has launched a very promising career.

Books by Regan Forest
HARLEQUIN TEMPTATION
80—THE ANSWERING TIDE

HARLEQUIN INTRIGUE
24—ONE STEP AHEAD

The Answering Tide

REGAN FOREST

Harlequin Books

TORONTO • NEW YORK • LONDON
AMSTERDAM • PARIS • SYDNEY • HAMBURG
STOCKHOLM • ATHENS • TOKYO • MILAN

To Cindy, with love

Published October 1985

ISBN 0-373-25180-7

1

WHY WOULD YOU never tell me, Mother?

Movements of clouds, splash of sun on giant silver wings, drone of engines. Adrienne Canaday's eyes moved away from the sky and down to her hands, folded across her lap. She stared at the scars on her left hand: three wide slashes resembling marks from a claw.

Secrets, Adrienne thought, as the fingers of her right hand brushed over the scars. There were always secrets, shadows of things unspoken. Dark whispers from gray caverns of time out of her memory's reach. Scars from lost years her mother couldn't or wouldn't explain.

From the window of the plane, Adrienne watched billows of white, runaway clouds roll against a lavender-blue sky. The gray, stiff Boston night seemed to have followed her, to wrap its fatigue and despair about her like a tangle of cobwebs. But now, finally, came the sun. Now, finally, another day was looming softly out of the darkness.

She shivered with the just-lived vision of her mother's flower-decked coffin. A helpless sob caught in her throat. The secrets, so long entombed in silence, were now entombed in stone. *Why would you never tell me, mother? Why would you never tell me who I am?*

Now others wanted to know. Like a sinister and skulking predator, the dark-clad attorney had appeared at the reading of the will to challenge her identity, pounce upon her legacy, in the name of strangers. How dared they! She was Laura Canaday's daugher, no matter what the obscure and grasping relatives claimed. And somehow she was going to prove it. There had to be a stone of truth still left unturned. Somewhere.

The San Diego skyline shone dimly beneath her. In the slanted frame of sunlight, wisps of Adrienne's hair frizzed white gold under the rim of her black straw hat. For her, this morning marked the dawn of new uncertainty. The black passion of grief had gradually given way to mourning, and then to the nagging ache of sorrow. Tears streaked her pale face. While the plane circled in its descent, Laura Canaday's sad, sweet presence wouldn't leave her.

If only it weren't too late, mother! If only we had talked just one last time....

Her cousin Carmen was there at the airport to meet her with a flurry of ebullient hugs and the news that Aunt Hester wasn't in town.

"It's better my mother isn't here, cuz," Carmen said, as she swung her yellow Triumph into the San Diego traffic. "That way there'll be no arguments about where you stay. It'll be with me, of course! You can't imagine our excitement about your visit! Isn't it awful that it took Laura's death to finally bring our family together again?"

Adrienne's pale-blue eyes were misting behind her sunglasses; she was so grateful for Carmen's bubbly welcome. "At the funeral I was thinking that we were eleven when your mother divorced Raleigh and left Boston. How could we have let fifteen years go by without seeing each other?"

"How could our mothers have let fifteen damn years go by—that's the sad part! What kind of sistership is that? Can you believe we've hit twenty-six, cuz? Twenty-six so soon? It's only the three of us now, but we're going to be a family again! I was so scared that with your concert coming up in New York you wouldn't come. I mean, all the work it must be finishing up your graduate degree. And wanting to be with your true love."

Carmen hadn't stopped smiling once since Adrienne's arrival, until now. She glanced at her cousin thoughtfully. "I don't like Richard Burroughs. A man too busy to attend the funeral of his fiancée's mother is automatically on my blacklist. What did busy Richard say about your trip to California? Hell, we won't be just the three of us after all, will we, if you and Richard have wedding plans?"

"There are no wedding plans."

"No? A long engagement, huh? That's great! Smart and great! You'll love my pad, cuz! I have an extra bedroom since my roommate lost her sanity and got married last month. We're only one block from Mission Bay. I've been making feverish plans!"

Adrienne felt, for the first time since her mother's death two weeks ago, as if she were surrounded by warmth. When Aunt Hester and Carmen had flown in only hours after Laura's unexpected death, arriving in Boston almost as quickly as she herself had been able to get there from New York, it had been as if they'd never left. Years of separation melted away in their shared grief, shared loss, and Adrienne was comforted to know she was not alone. She had a family, almost forgotten, who had come to her at once, and begged her to come back into their lives.

And now, desperately, she needed them. In this California morning that shimmered as bright and warm as Carmen, she needed them. And the sea air was filled with freedom, which she also needed. Freedom from tradition and from the stiff dictates of society she had accepted all her life.

Now here was the sun. She gazed out the car windows as they sped through traffic. "Why didn't Aunt Hester tell me she was going away? She knew I came specifically to talk to her."

"Oh, she'll be back in a few days. She's always hopping down to Acapulco with friends. I think she needed time to gather her wits after hearing about those shirt-tail relations trying to take your inheritance from you. I don't know when I've seen mother so furious. How did Sir Richard take the news?"

"Richard was afraid his parents and the distinguished law firm of Burroughs, Markson and Burroughs couldn't accept his marrying an impoverished mongrel waif."

Carmen turned, wide-eyed. The car swerved and a horn honked. She struggled back into her lane. "Richard couldn't have said that! No one in the twentieth century has ever said anything like that!"

"He may have worded it a bit more eloquently, but—" her jaw tightened with hurt that was building itself into ragged anger "—but not much. When I told him on the phone that these Indiana relations claimed to have proof my birth documents were forgeries, I may as well have said my mother found me in a garbage can wrapped in a newspaper. Heaven help us! Imagine the possibility that I may have the blood of beggars in my veins! Richard acted as if he were the one who needed to be comforted! I'd just come from my attorney's office, feeling more alone than I'd ever felt in my life, and all he could talk about was his parents' reaction to this...this apparent conspiracy of my mother's to keep my real identity a secret." She trembled, even in the warmth of the car. "I realized with a horrid jolt that it was a moment of immutable change, and told Richard not to lose any sleep over it. Or over me. Ever."

Her cousin smiled crookedly. "Does this mean your engagement is off?"

Adrienne laughed. It seemed unbelievable to be laughing about it, but Carmen's mischievous humor always could touch her.

"What a fool he is! And he jumped the gun, cuz! You haven't lost anything yet."

"Yes, I have. I've lost Richard."

"It sounds to me as if that loss is a gain in thin disguise. Thank goodness you didn't marry him before you discovered the feathers growing under his custom-tailored suits." She glanced sideways. "I don't believe he called you a 'mongrel.'"

"No. Richard is delicate. He'd choke on the word *mongrel. Sordid* is a Richard-style word. He called the contesting of the will 'sordid.'" She closed her eyes, trying to shut away the hurt.

Carmen's voice softened. "I'm sorry, Adrienne. I really am."

"Don't be. The Burroughs approved of Richard's marrying an heiress, and they were receptive to the idea of his bride's being a concert pianist. But as for the question of my blood! The dutiful son never got up nerve enough to tell his parents I was adopted. Can you believe it? I'd have been miserable in that family. It took Richard's off-guard panic to make me understand what they really are."

"Well, it should be some comfort to know that eighty-six point seven percent of all marriages in millionaire brackets either last only for convenience or end in divorce. See what misery you've been saved from?"

Adrienne grinned. "Eighty-six point seven, huh?"

"Right." Carmen paused. "You've been doing some soul-searching, haven't you?"

"Till my brain aches. I've made up my mind I want to find out who I am, Carmen, not just for the inheritance. Who I am may not affect a judge's decision in the least if the adoption was illegal. But I want to know why there is such secrecy about my past. I hope Aunt Hester can help. She's got to know *something*."

"If she does, she never gave a hint of it to me."

Waiting at a traffic light, Carmen flashed a careless smile at her cousin. "Maybe you're French! You look like a Paris model. You were a porcelain doll when you were a kid, and I was so jealous! And you're still a porcelain doll. When I heard about the contested will so soon after the shock of Laura's death, my first thought was that you were so fragile you'd come apart over this. And now this thing with Richard. But your appearance deceives, cuz. You're weathering all this pretty well. You're not as fragile as you look, are you?"

Not feeling the same confidence, Adrienne returned the smile and wondered if the lost-in-limbo feeling inside her came under the heading of fragile.

"You're just pale as hell, that's all," Carmen continued. "A little California sun will do wonders for you.

But with skin as fair as yours, we don't dare overdo it. You'll need proper playclothes, starting with a wide-brimmed hat. We'll do some shopping in Pacific Beach before we go over to Sea World this afternoon."

"'Sea World'?"

"Yep! While you're my guest you're going to forget dark halls of museums and art galleries. Forget symphonies and ballets. Oh, don't get me wrong, cuz. I still haven't got over the fact that my very own relative is a budding concert pianist. In New York! I've bragged to anyone who would listen, including the entire staff of the school where I teach and half the kids. But I want you to have a taste of my world for a change—the zoo, the beach, hidden-away old seafood restaurants, boats. My boyfriend Scotty has a sailboat we play with every weekend on the bay. Does it sound okay?"

"It sounds just terrific."

The brunette let out a joyous whoop, her short hair standing straight up in the breeze. "Adrienne, we're together again! We shouldn't have been apart all these years just because our mothers lived in separate worlds. But we'll make up for it!" She pounded the steering wheel with the palm of her hand. "This is so exciting! I have my main relative back!"

THAT MORNING, in a sea lab upshore from San Diego, Kendall Burke had been at work since sunrise.

He resembled a statue of a pagan god, with his nearly naked, golden body silhouetted against sunlight, his hair blowing gently in his eyes, his arms raised above his head. Beneath him the surface of the water dimpled dark and bright, shimmering in sparkles of morning sun. Squinting in the glare, his tired, stinging eyes followed the underwater shadow of a swimming dolphin.

In response to the hand signals of her trainer, the dolphin circled the pool, then raised her silver head and tossed a plastic disk into a hanging basket. Turning swiftly, she dived, then surfaced on the opposite side, near the computer station.

"Perfect!" Kendall called. "Perfect, Aphrodite!"

He lowered himself from the platform into the water to praise the animal with loving strokes. A second dolphin swam closer, but not close enough to participate in the touching. "Come over here, Ulysses!" the man urged, but the huge animal only sent out some clicks and kept his distance.

The cold water, the excitement of a job well done and the familiar, bewitching feel of smooth cetacean skin combined to make Kendall forget his fatigue. Aphrodite's mysterious, intelligent eyes followed his movements, conveying friendship, tolerance, trust and, as always, filling him with wonder.

Brian Palmer, assistant director of the Pacific Laboratory for Cetacean Communications Studies, strolled to the edge of the pool. He plopped himself down and, dangling his feet in the water, watched the lab's director cavort with the dolphin. "That was fantastic, Ken! You're communicating in sentences with no confusion whatever. Aphrodite's comprehension of your triple signals is faster than mine." He began unwrapping a candy bar. "Why didn't you tell me you'd be up and out here this early?"

Kendall continued to stroke the dolphin, who was nudging him playfully, ignoring the circling of the large male, who raised his beaklike snout each time he swam near. "I didn't plan to start so early. Worked most of the night on the computer program and journal notes. Then when I saw the sun coming up, I figured it was too late to go to bed."

"So you've been up all night. You look it. Why the devil do you push yourself like that?"

"Maybe I'm an insomniac. There's just so damned much on my mind."

The dolphin squeaked a Delphic comment, as if she were in total agreement.

"Aphrodite is so interested in the work now that Ulysses doesn't distract her as much as before." Ken returned the conversation to the dolphins.

Sun gleamed on Brian Palmer's tan, balding head. His feet made melodic little splashes against the water—nervous splashes. He chewed the chocolate bar vigorously. "You don't take time to open the mail, either. If you'd opened yesterday's mail you'd have had another reason for losing a night's sleep. The government grant didn't come through. We're in big trouble."

Kendall's dark-blue eyes clouded. He squinted up at the man in tense silence. Giving the dolphin a departing pat, he raised his muscular body from the pool and sat dripping on the concrete beside his colleague, pushing his wet hair back from his forehead. "Dammit, Brian. Are you sure?"

"Yep. We're squashed. A hundred thousand dollars worth of electronic equipment on order, and not a dime to pay for any of it. We may have to close down."

"We can't!" Kendall's fists clenched. He stood and began to pace. Palm branches cast moving shadows across his handsome face, light and dark shadows, reflecting his sudden change of mood. "We're so close to a breakthrough—right on the edge of it, Brian! We can't quit now!"

"We might reconsider working with the navy."

"And chance the possibility of military exploitation of the dolphins? No bloody way!"

"Okay! Calm down. We both agree on that. But what ideas have you got?"

"I'll get an advance on another book. It'll be enough to keep us from sinking right away."

Brian wadded up the candy wrapper and wiped his mustache. He looked away from the eyes of the younger man to the two dolphins splashing at the far side of the pool. "When will you have time to write another book?"

"I'll just have to find time in the evenings."

Brian scowled. "I'm not sure I like what's been happening with you these past few months, Ken. Here you are, what? Thirty-three? Thirty-four? And I'll bet you can't remember what a social life is—unless you have a damn good memory. Don't you know what they say about all work and no play?"

Kendall picked up a hose and began spraying the salt from the protective shield of glass in front of the computer equipment. "Ken is already a dull boy."

"An obsessed boy!" Brian squinted through the spray of water from the hose, a splash of jewels in the reflection of the sun's rays. "I'm ten years older than you and measurably uglier. I may be just as dedicated to our work, but I'm not buried in it to my eyeballs! At least I date!"

"I've got too much to do right now. We're fighting for survival here. There'll be time to play when we've survived."

"Ha! When we've survived this crisis—if we survive this crisis—you'll have bigger and greater projects already started. Face it, Ken, some of your friends are holding memorial services, thinking you died. Do you even see your son anymore?"

"I drove to San Fernando last weekend for his thirteenth birthday. I see Jeff as often as I can."

Brian, noting the clenched jaw and a touch of warning in his friend's voice, backed off. His tone lightened. "How's your kid doing?"

"He's doing great. His stepfather is all the things I wasn't—a good provider, fine husband and father..." Ken's voice softened until it had blended with the sound of water spattering against the glass. He was taking longer than was necessary to wash the screen.

Brian rose. "Yeah, well, you're not much good at being a free-spirited bachelor, either. You may have your recognition as one of the country's top authorities on dolphins, but it comes at the cost of isolating yourself from humans."

"It's what's important to me. Hell, you know how important it is to mankind to find a way of communicating with another species, especially a sea-dwelling species. It's staggering to think about what we could learn from the cetaceans."

"It's *all* you think about!"

"Okay, it is. I admit it." Ken turned off the hose and walked toward his friend, stenciling wet footprints on the sun-dried concrete. Affectionately he touched the shorter man's shoulder, his burst of anger gone, his need to be defensive melted in the knowledge that Brian's concern was one of friendship, of caring. "Let's go over to the Sea Cliff. I'll buy you breakfast."

"Well," Brian said with a grin, "that's at least a start at a human social encounter."

"We can discuss the new computer signals over eggs and coffee."

"Swell."

"Aphrodite was showing more interest in the computer this morning, did you notice?"

"Oh, yeah, it's all swell." The older man's voice was rough and dark, his eyes cautious and despairing. "All great! And when we've learned to talk with the dolphins, is anyone besides us going to listen to them? Will the world accept it, Ken? Will they believe us?"

"Now who's being the cynic? There are those who will listen."

The men walked from the pool to the main building of the laboratory with worry over their financial problems moving them closer to the borders of defeat.

"Hell, they won't even listen long enough to put our grant money through," Brian challenged. "All these mysterious others who believe we can communicate intellectually with the dolphins—where the devil are they?"

"Sooner or later," Ken answered, "they'll find us."

2

AT FIRST IT WAS THEIR EYES that stunned her. How could such alien eyes seem so familiar? Bright, wakeful sparks of mystery rose up from the world of water to meet her. From her place at the edge of the dolphin petting pool at Sea World, Adrienne stared hypnotically at the animals cavorting in the water. Excitement thumped inside her. These strangely smiling, beaked faces—how mysteriously compelling they were! Without conscious awareness of her actions, she extended her arms to them.

Her gaze fixed on a single eye across the pool, an eye that met hers, unblinking. For a moment the dolphin stared. Then it swam toward her, raising its big head as it neared. From somewhere in unfathomed depths of her being, Adrienne heard the sounds of the ocean, the ebb and flood of sea tides. The dolphin slid up onto the underwater shelf directly in front of her.

Her breath caught at the nearness of the sleek, massive gray body. Some incarnate, awesome emotion held her suspended in time and space. In a half trance, she reached out to touch the dolphin. Silkiness like the feel of dew on soft new leaves, smoothness like rain on glass, roused in her an excitement beyond all reason.

There was a small crowd along the rails of the petting pool. People were dangling freshly purchased dead fish over the water to entice the sea mammals to the sides. The pool contained several species, but only one, the bottle-nosed dolphin, swam directly to Adrienne, as if it were greeting an old friend.

While Adrienne petted the dolphin, lost in enchantment unlike any she had ever known, Carmen leaned over the side of the pool and into the shadow of Adrienne's wide-brimmed white hat. "Hey, are you wearing fish-oil perfume, or what? That dolphin acts like it knows you!"

Still stroking the silver head, Adrienne glanced at her cousin. "I don't know what's going on, Carmen. I feel I've been here before, like I've known dolphins before, but I've never seen one in my life, except in pictures."

Carmen stepped back, raising her camera to her eye. "Let's get this on film. In Boston they'll never believe this—you petting dolphins! After all, only point one-eight-four-seven-nine people in the entire world have ever actually touched a dolphin!"

"Why do you have such a preposterous statistic committed to memory?"

"Statistics fascinate me."

"I've noticed."

The water swayed with the movement of swimming animals, while the bottle-nosed dolphin with the friendly eyes remained on the ledge beside Adrienne. In bright reflections of sun on water, she gazed down at her own hand stroking the dolphin's head. The moving water waved back and forth over the phantom, clawlike scars on her hand, mesmerizing her, bringing to her mind the wild, haunting song of the ocean.

It came over her again, and stronger: the sensation that she had been here before, touched these dolphins before. But, no! Impossible. It must have been a dream.

Yes, a dream. She had dreamed of dolphins sometimes when she was a child. Her mother liked to tell her stories of the sea and dolphins, and afterward she would dream of meeting dolphins out in open sea. Now the act of seeing them, touching them for the first time, became a mystical resurrection of those dreams.

Minutes passed—minutes lost to time and to disturbing hints of something more—some memory or some dream just out of reach. When Carmen finally succeeded in tugging her away from the pool, with wails about a hundred attractions left to see, Adrienne turned back once to the dark fins sliding through the water. A sensation of sadness rippled through her. So fascinated was she with the dolphins, she had to force herself to turn away and leave them.

THE FOLLOWING AFTERNOON—a sky-blue Sunday with light breezes blowing off the sea—Carmen's yellow Triumph turned off the coast highway onto Aspen Drive, a narrow, paved road that wound over two miles of hilly terrain. They were climbing; the blue water of the Pacific was below them. Adrienne looked out at the view of the ocean through tall trees.

She sat forward. "I appreciate your driving all the way up here, Carmen."

"You want to see more dolphins I'll find you dolphins! Keep a lookout for the sign."

"It's Sunday." Adrienne brushed back blowing white-blond curls from her eyes. "Maybe there's no one here. Or maybe the public isn't allowed at this lab."

"There should be somebody here. I'm sure they'll let us look around." She slowed the car. "Is that it over there?"

"No, that sign says the Sea Cliff. It looks like a country estate that's been converted to a restaurant. There's a small sign on your side...that's it! Pacific Laboratory for Cetacean Communications Studies."

Carmen turned onto a one-lane road and drove a quarter mile farther under high old eucalyptus trees before the flat red roofs of buildings came into view. The land sloped, then flattened into the green lawns of an area enclosed by a chain-link fence. Inside were low, white buildings scattered between three shimmering pools of water, one of which was enormous.

A gate was open. Beyond it only two vehicles, a small car and a pickup truck, stood side by side and alone in the parking area. Carmen pulled up alongside them and turned off the engine. A heavy silence fell from the tops of the tall trees like mist. There were the sounds of birds singing, and in the distance, below them, was the steady, even breathing of the ocean.

The largest building, labeled Office, was locked. "Let's just walk around and see what we can find," Carmen suggested.

"Wouldn't it have been easier just to go back to the Sea World petting pool?"

"It's too crowded there. If you're really serious about wanting to learn more about dolphins, this would be the place."

"Well, crowded it's not! There doesn't seem to be anybody around."

"Yeah, there is." She pointed. "Over there by the big pool."

Squinting under the rim of her hat, Adrienne could see the figure of a man kneeling over the water. Carmen stepped up her pace. They walked over a wide sidewalk between stretches of green lawn. Adrienne saw splashing in the pool. Dolphins! The thundering began in her breast once again, an excitement she could neither explain nor contain. Sucking in her breath, she asked, "What do you think he's doing?"

"Talking to dolphins, I guess. That's what they're supposed to do here."

The path sloped down and then upward to the pool. They saw that there were two men, one by the water, the other sitting across the pool in front of a machine, both so absorbed in whatever they were doing that they had not seen the strangers approach. The man by the pool was tossing small objects like coins into the water and giving hand signals to a dolphin, while a second dolphin floated at the side, simply watching.

They were within ten feet of the pool, when the working dolphin turned from its trainer abruptly, emitted a series of beeps and swam toward the edge where the two women were approaching.

"What the hell?" the man exclaimed as he straightened.

Adrienne halted, intimidated by the sound of the man's voice. Something was wrong.

A second voice, that of the dolphin, clicked at her. At *her!* With the dolphin's high-pitched greeting, flaps of all reality folded away into floating wings of lost and swollen time. Pure wonder incited in her an almost-uncrontrollable urge to rush toward the animal and touch it. But at the same time, there were vibrations just as strong coming from the other side of her, and these vibrations, in contrast, were definitely not welcoming. Uneasily she turned from the dolphin, to face a man so startlingly handsome that several runaway seconds passed before she was fully aware of the ice-blue anger in his staring eyes.

It was as impossible to look directly into those blue eyes as it was to stare into midday sun. Adrienne lowered her eyes quickly, but to a view almost as blinding.

The man was nearly naked. His low-waisted jeans shorts were torn on one side, revealing a portion of hip muscle. Had the shorts been any shorter, there would have been little point in wearing them at all. Had they been any tighter, he might have suffered bodily injury. His muscular body, with the one exception of the partly exposed buttock, was tanned deep, golden brown.

Why was Carmen so uncharacteristically silent? Did it have something to do with those shorts? Adrienne forced her eyes upward—over the mat of curly, sun-bleached hair on the man's chest, up to the hostile eyes again—eyes deep set under thick brows. His forehead was creased in a frown.

"What did you do?" His voice was so deep it seemed to have an echo.

Adrienne flushed and hesitated. He was staring at her exclusively and not at Carmen, and she wondered if he had some way of knowing she was the one who had distracted his dolphin. She had no way of knowing it herself, but she was certain just the same. She turned away from the accusing eyes. "I'm sorry if we interrupted something important."

The man's brow smoothed somewhat after her breathy, soft-voiced apology. "What did you do to get the dolphin's attention? When she's working she's rarely distracted by anything."

Carmen was smiling pastily at the older man, who had left his post at the machines and was fast approaching them. This was all very embarrassing, and Adrienne was beginning to regret having talked so incessantly about the dolphins that Carmen had looked up this place in order to please her. They shouldn't have come. But here they were, wreaking havoc in record time.

"It's not Adrienne's fault," Carmen cooed in her sweetest, most helpless voice. "The same thing happened at Sea World yesterday. When the dolphins saw her they came right over to her."

The shorter man looked to Adrienne like an aging, rather battered James Bond. Also deeply tanned, he wore sunglasses, a white T-shirt and shorts, and had a mustache. No smile. "What happened?" he asked. "What's going on?"

His colleague answered with thin sarcasm, "It appears Aphrodite has guests. She stopped working to say hello."

Unable to hide her discomfort, Adrienne said lamely, "We didn't intend to interfere." Why was it necessary for the man to be so rude? Couldn't he see they were sorry?

The older man apparently could see it. He managed a grin. "Aphrodite wouldn't show any interest in reporters. We've learned that. So what are you, trainers? Spies, maybe?" He had begun to stare at Adrienne. "You don't look like a trainer."

"No," she said defensively, wondering if the man was joking about the spy part. "I never saw a dolphin in my life until yesterday."

The men exchanged skeptical glances. Obviously they were unconvinced. Her embarrassment deepened, even while the one who looked like a used James Bond continued to smile. "Is there something we can do for you, ladies?"

No one could ask a favor of these men. The handsome one not only didn't smile, he was wearing an expression that came suspiciously close to a genuine pout. Adrienne resented that, along with his insinuation that she had done something disruptive on purpose.

She thrust her hands into the pockets of her shorts and took a step back to distance herself from them. In the pool, both dolphins had come to the side and lay in the water wearing their perpetual smiles, as if they were eavesdropping and enjoying the human encounter. At least someone was amused! At the nearness of the dolphins, Adrienne's pulse quickened. Depression fell over her like a cloak. How could she and Carmen have blown it like this?

"I wanted to see dolphins," she explained, forcing herself to meet the younger man's hostile eyes. Oh, those eyes! It took almost superhuman willpower to keep her voice steady and clear. "We heard you are experimenting in human-dolphin communication, and we...I...hoped to learn something about it and to... to...well, to watch the dolphins, if it's allowed."

Accepting her cue, Carmen extended her hand and smiled. "I'm Carmen Janssen. This is Adrienne Canaday, Boston relative on tour. I have assured her that

Californians are a hospitable breed *au total*, so don't you guys make a liar out of me, okay? As I told you, Adrienne had this incredible experience at the petting pool yesterday with two dolphins who looked just like these. She was excited as hell about it, so we made a wish, closed our eyes and found ourselves standing here, apologizing for something your dolphin just did. Whatever the devil it was."

The handsome one was staring again; Adrienne felt the penetration of the hard, blue eyes. He said, "Tell me about the incredible experience."

She colored. "Carmen already told you. They saw me and came to me. The way it happened here just now."

"You must have done something."

"How could I? I don't know the first thing about dolphins!"

"She doesn't have cod-liver-oil breath, if that's what you're thinking," Carmen muttered.

This made him smile. It wasn't much of a smile, but it provided a clue that he might be human, and it softened the stiff line of the most sensual male lips Adrienne had seen in her life. He asked, "What were you thinking about?"

Had he just read her thoughts about his sensual lips? Adrienne's cheeks burned. "What was I thinking about when?"

"When you saw the dolphins." His deep voice had become impatient again, and she remembered she had interfered with his work.

She glanced down at his perfectly proportioned body, then back up to meet his eyes in a second challenging stare. Something in his steady gaze conveyed sincerity behind his strange question; for some reason he actually was interested in what she had been thinking about at the petting pool.

"I was feeling very emotional about the dolphins. Seeing them for the first time really stirred me. I thought about them all day and all night. It's hard to describe, just a sort of...instant love."

Oddly he didn't flinch at the word. "And here? Were you feeling the same thing here when you saw them?"

"Yes. But what does it matter what I was thinking about? Dolphins aren't mind readers, are they?"

"Sometimes I think they are. Through sonar and echolocation, they can penetrate the body through sound waves, so they're probably experts at reading emotions. In my personal opinion, it goes further than that. I believe there is a higher-than-sixth-sense communication. But I can't prove it."

"You mean you think they were responding to my thoughts?"

"Your feelings, more likely. The vibrations you were emitting must have been incredibly strong."

"Yes, they were strong. It was a feeling of. . .of kinship."

The clicking of the dolphins, asking for attention, made her turn to the pool. "Would they let me touch them?"

"Ulysses, the big one, wouldn't. I'm not sure about the female, but I rather doubt it. She isn't used to many humans, won't even get too chummy with Brian here unless her mood is right." He wiped his hand across his perspiring forehead and acted restless, as if he were in a hurry for the two women to leave.

"Don't act like the troll under the bridge, Ken," the older man said, smiling more easily than before. "Let's see what happens." He extended his hand. "Apologies. We both have rotten manners. My name is Brian Palmer. The troll is Kendall Burke, world authority on dolphins, best-selling author and pacesetter for fashionable beachwear, as evidenced by his present ensemble."

Kendall Burke's eyes dropped to glimpse his cutoffs. A half-embarrassed expression crossed his face and he turned slightly to move the revealing rip from the women's direct line of vision.

Adrienne handed her wide-brimmed hat to Carmen and followed Brian Palmer to the pool edge. She knelt, pressing her knees against the rough cement. The smaller dolphin responded to her outstretched hand at once, rubbing against her with a slow, graceful slide.

"Look at this, Ken!" Brian said. "Did you ever see Aphrodite in such a social mood?"

"No," he admitted. "Even old Ulysses acts interested. Ordinarily he'd be at the other end of the pool by now."

"Ulysses is not a friendly dolphin," Brian explained to Adrienne. "We don't even try to train him. He's just here as an observer." He stood behind her, making no attempt to get any nearer to the dolphin himself. "This species is called tursiops, by the way. Bottle-nosed dolphins. It's the type you usually see in performing shows."

"Are they more intelligent than other species?"

"No, but they're easy to work with, and they can adjust better to shallow water and warmer temperatures than most other species. In the wild, tursiops tend to live closer to shore."

Brian backed away slowly and began a half-whispered conversation with Carmen. Kendall moved forward to observe Adrienne's rapport with Aphrodite. He didn't say anything, just watched her as she stroked the smooth, silver-gray head, but his closeness unnerved her, for she was beginning to realize she reacted to this man in much the same way she reacted to the dolphins—with instant fascination. Maybe it was his close association with dolphins. Ah, who was she trying to kid? Those indecently tight shorts that caused her pulse to quicken had very little to do with the man's occupation!

He knelt beside her, still silent, apparently absorbed in private thoughts. The dolphin moved against Adrienne's arm. Kendall remained so quiet that these moments with the dolphin began to lull Adrienne, to pull her back to that mysterious song again—the song of ocean, the feel of water, the nearness of a kindred soul.

She was unaware of how much time had elapsed while she knelt there next to this strange, silent man, stroking the dolphin. Brian and Carmen were talking behind her, but she hadn't heard any of their conversation. Finally, because she felt she ought to, she stood up reluctantly. So did Kendall. The dolphin floated a small distance away, but continued to watch Adrienne.

Suddenly, with no warning whatever, Aphrodite leaped into the air and brought her flukes down on the surface of the water with a heavy slap. Carmen and Brian stepped back quickly, but Adrienne and Kendall were soaked by a fountain of spray. She let out an involuntary squeal.

He turned to her with a very odd grin. "I'm in the water with Aphrodite so much, I guess she doesn't realize that some of us land creatures prefer to stay dry."

He didn't seem to mind in the least that water was dripping from his face and his hair. Carelessly he brushed back brown-and-gold-streaked curls from his eyes as if nothing important had happened.

She raged inside herself. If it was so unimportant, why was he staring at her, staring almost through her? She glanced down to confirm what she feared: everything beneath her soaked white shorts and blouse was clearly visible. And Carmen was giggling, damn her!

Adrienne pulled at the once-crisp blouse and held it away from her breasts. The water was cold. Brian found a towel on a nearby bench and handed it to her, and as he did, she noticed he was giving Kendall Burke strange looks, the kind of silent reprimand one gives a misbehaving child in front of guests. That didn't seem fair. After all, Kendall hadn't been the one who soaked her, and he was just as wet. Brian must have noticed the indecent way Kendall had stared at her breasts. Maybe Mr. Burke himself was feeling guilty about it, because he seemed to be deliberately avoiding Brian's eyes, just the way the misbehaving child would do.

She dried her face and hair, and still the older man looked at the younger one with a disapproving scowl when he thought Adrienne was hidden behind the towel and didn't notice.

She said, "I think we've interrupted your work long enough."

"Feel free to look around," Kendall offered, directing the invitation to Carmen. "There are dolphins in the other pools."

Adrienne tried to smile. She was shivering.

"Keep the towel," Brian said. "You'll be cold without it."

"We will look around, since it's okay," Carmen told them cheerfully. She could afford to be cheerful, Adrienne thought. She was dry.

"If you have any questions, you know where to find us."

Adrienne looked down at her shorts. The patterns of lace on her underpants were clearly visible through her wet shorts. More than the lace was visible, for all she knew. Backing slowly away from the men, she wished the towel were larger. "We won't interrupt again," she muttered meekly.

Carmen followed her cousin down the slope from the pool. "What's your hurry, cuz?"

"You can look at me and ask that?"

She grinned. "I wish I looked that good wet."

"Carmen, I feel uncomfortable around that man! He was mad at me for mucking up his work."

"Maybe a little. I got the feeling he wasn't too comfortable around you, either."

"There should be a law against men with his looks running around without any more clothes than he was wearing."

Carmen laughed. "You got that wrong, cuz. There should be a law preventing hunks like him from wearing anything at all!"

Adrienne shivered in her damp clothes, even though the sun was warm and in midafternoon there was little breeze. "Let's get out of here! I don't want to look around. I don't understand anything that just happened."

From the top of the little hill, they looked back to the pool. Kendall was in the water with the dolphins.

Adrienne sighed as if she were in pain. "Oh, he's so lucky, Carmen! Imagine swimming with dolphins, being with them every day! Just think how much he must know about them! I've never envied anyone so much in my life!"

"I know how you feel, cuz. I felt the same way when I saw how that man looked at you.

"He was angry!"

"No, I don't think so. I think it was something else."

WHEN KENDALL CAME OUT OF THE SHOWER in his small apartment at the back of the main building of the laboratory complex, Brian was sitting on the couch with a beer, waiting for him. Wearing only a towel, Ken took a beer from the refrigerator and sat down.

"Why did you do it, Ken?"

"Do what?"

"Did you want her to leave that badly? I can't believe you're lecherous enough to anticipate the sight of that woman's body through her soaked clothes!"

"I don't know what you're talking about."

"Like hell you don't! I saw you give that signal to Aphrodite. You did it on purpose!"

Ken took a long drink from the can of beer and was silent. There was a half smile on his face.

"Why, Ken?"

He shrugged weakly. "She was making me uneasy. There is something mysterious about that woman and the way the dolphins react to her."

"You're the only imbecile I know who would go to such extremes to drive away a beautiful lady."

Kendall's expression changed. "She is beautiful. Almost too beautiful."

"So that's it! You're scared! Scared you might get distracted like the dolphins!"

He stared at his beer can, his eyes half-closed. "Maybe."

"You're nuts, Ken!" Brian removed his glasses and wiped his eyes as if they stung. "All they wanted was a little information and a look at the dolphins. You had no reason to—"

Ken jumped from the chair, spilling beer over his hand. "I don't know why I did it and I feel guilty enough without your help, dammit!"

"Okay. Okay! It's not that big a deal. I just can't figure you out sometimes, that's all."

Ken tossed the towel aside and pulled on a pair of faded jeans. He didn't bother with underwear. "You figured me out perfectly just a minute ago. The woman had me completely distracted from the second I turned around and saw her standing there. I couldn't help myself, and I suppose I resented her for it."

"That doesn't even make sense!"

"Nothing made sense from the minute they walked up today." He switched on a radio, and soft strains of music filled the small room. Grabbing his beer, he moved to the refrigerator, took out a chunk of cheese and sliced it sloppily with a dull knife, popping bites into his mouth and tapping his foot to the music. "She's a very classy lady, Brian. Maybe that's what I resented."

"What you were scared of, you mean."

"Okay. What I was scared of."

Brian scowled as he crushed his empty can with one hand. Ken knew from the look on his friend's face that this wouldn't make any sense to Brian, either—his not wanting a woman like Adrienne Canaday in his life.

But he didn't, not even for an hour. In a day or an hour or a moment, a woman like Adrienne could turn a guy's orderly world upside down. It wasn't going to happen to him. Not again. He had too much to lose. And so did she.

3

THIRTEEN LEAFY GREEN PLANTS hung from the ceiling of Carmen's sunny kitchen in Pacific Beach. Above a round glass dining table was a big corner window with a view, through palm branches, of a courtyard below. Beyond, over roofs of shorter apartment buildings, sparkled the blue waters of Mission Bay.

On Wednesday morning, after an unexpected call from Hester, Adrienne and Carmen sat at the glass table, drinking their third cups of coffee.

Carmen looked up at her rooster-shaped wall clock. "Mother isn't expecting you for an hour. We have time for another cup."

"I'm not used to so much caffeine."

"You'll need it to meet mother's energy level. She's all worked up over these obscure Indiana relations of Geoffrey Canaday going after your rightful legacy. After all, Laura was Geoffrey Canaday's widow for over thirty years!"

Adrienne sighed, dreading this meeting with her Aunt Hester. For a few crazy, sunny days with Carmen, she had forgotten the whole grim legal battle, and it was hard to have to think about it now, with the sun so bright outside and the palm branches swaying lazily and Sea World just across the bay....

The coffee maker gurgled loudly; fresh coffee aroma filled the bright room. Adrienne rose in response. "I had a dream about dolphins last night. The dream was so real. I was in the ocean swimming with them and they were all around me, and Kendall Burke swam up, wearing diving gear, and told me I wasn't supposed to be there. But then when he took off the scuba mask, it wasn't Kendall. It was a stranger."

Carmen's wide, dark eyes followed Adrienne's hands as she poured coffee carefully into each mug. "Do you realize you haven't talked about anything but dolphins all week? I thought that maybe when mother was home you'd get your mind back on why you came out here to California in the first place."

Adrienne replaced the coffeepot and sat down again. "I can't help it, Carmen. I keep thinking about Ken in the water with them and how I envied him. I want to swim with the dolphins. Just once! The idea has been smoldering until I can't stand it anymore. I close my eyes and see those crazy, smiling faces. I hear those funny sounds they make. Sometimes it's as if they're trying to tell me something, and I can almost understand, but I can't understand."

"Have you made up your mind about going back to the lab?"

"I want to so much, but I'm afraid to."

"You're afraid of him, is what you mean. If you ask me, it's Kendall Burke you can't get out of your mind."

"All right, I plead guilty to that, too. What was it about that guy?"

Her cousin blew small vapors of steam from her coffee cup. "Other than an incredibly handsome face and a body that ought to be a sculpture, I can't imagine!"

"He isn't that good-looking."

"He is when he smiles."

"He doesn't do much smiling, does he? Do you think Brian Palmer was telling the truth about Ken being a world authority on dolphins?"

"Sure. I have the feeling that if you were a dolphin you'd have him hand-feeding you dead fish by now. Why don't you do what you're dying to do—go back out there and ask him if you can swim with his dolphins?"

"He's not the most approachable man in the world."

Carmen slowly stirred more sugar into her cup. Adrienne noticed she seemed to be doing more playing with her coffee than drinking it.

"Burke's not married, in case you're wondering."

"How do you know?"

"Because Scotty told me."

Adrienne's eyebrows raised. "Oh, did he?"

Carmen nodded. "Scotty has a friend who knows somebody who works at Sea World, who knows a lot about Mr. Burke. He—Kendall, that is—has been divorced for several years. He has a son somewhere. I was curious, so I asked around." She paused under Adrienne's disapproving stare. "It was the way he looked at you, cuz! There was something strange going on. You knew it and I knew it. I wanted to find out who he is, that's all."

Adrienne sipped coffee slowly, her eyes fixed on a green branch outside the window where a small brown bird was singing praises to the morning. "When I think rationally about it, it's a ridiculous thing to ask him—to let me get in the water with the dolphins. He'd probably say no."

"But you're going to try."

"Yes," she heard her own voice answer.

Carmen grinned broadly. "You've really changed, Adrienne. When we were kids, you were terrified of the water. We couldn't get you near a swimming pool."

"Mother worked hard to help me get over that phobia. She even hired the world's most patient swim instructor. It took years."

"Your mother must have been remarkable. I remember her as being very quiet and dignified—always listening to symphonies or painting landscapes or arranging flowers, wearing dark silk dresses trimmed in lace. But she must have had a strong and cunning side to her, too. I'll bet there was nothing on earth she wouldn't have done for you. She shielded you with her life, I think, more than any of us ever knew."

A small mist of tears appeared in Adrienne's light-blue eyes. "There were so many things I never knew. But mother told me in a million ways how much she loved me."

After some moments of silence, Carmen leaned back in her chair. "I know why you've avoided the subject of your fake birth certificate. You're afraid to talk to my mother, aren't you? Afraid of what you might find out."

"Yes. I didn't realize it until Aunt Hester phoned. Now suddenly it can't be put off any longer. Whatever reason mother had for all the secrecy it can't have been anything good, can it? I mean, people only guard secrets when they're hiding something from the world."

Carmen glanced uncomfortably at the clock again. "Well, let's face this like Roman warriors. Are you ready to go? I'll drop you over there and do some shopping while you and mother talk."

"Thanks, Roman warrior, that's mighty brave of you."

"Do you want me to stay there with you?"

"No," Adrienne conceded. "This is something I'd better do alone."

"I can't stand to see you get your hopes up, when this may be just a ghost hunt, cuz. You have to keep in mind that only six point three percent of all orphans ever succeed in finding their blood roots."

"I'll keep that in mind," Adrienne promised as she pushed away from the table, trying to ignore the spring of fear coiling through her. *Ghost hunt?* She wished Carmen had chosen different words.

HESTER TIPTON, slender, lavishly jeweled and wearing raspberry silk, sat opposite her niece. The tea ceremony was turning out exactly as Adrienne had anticipated—unchanged from the days of her childhood. A silver tray on a dark carved tea cart and Aunt Hester perched, straight-shouldered on the edge of a Queen Anne chair, a lace-edged napkin over her knee, pouring tea into thin, white china cups.

The room was no surprise, either. Very large oil paintings, some of which her mother had painted and which Adrienne could remember from years ago, blended richly with antique furnishings. It was so like the Boston house. She couldn't imagine Aunt Hester living in any other surroundings.

Hester handed her a delicate teacup set on a matching silver-rimmed saucer. "Your telephone call shocked us, Adrienne. How dare these people question your right to your inheritance? Did they think I would sit back and let that happen?" She wrinkled her nose. "I've consulted my attorneys. Some way or other we'll find a way to stop them.

"Your mother and I made a pact when you and Carmen were small. We agreed to leave everything to our daughters, none to each other. It was to be stipulated in both wills that if either you or Carmen should die before you received your inheritance, the entire estate of one girl would go to the other. Laura stuck by that agreement. It never occurred to either of us there were these vultures hanging about the fringes of our lives. Yet it is strange that Laura would have left any legal matters open to question. It wasn't her style. And if she did, she must have had a very good reason."

Adrienne's cup clicked gently against its saucer as she set it down. "Aunt Hester, I was hoping you could tell me what that reason was. You were living in Boston when mother adopted me, and the two of you were close then."

The older woman's eyes darkened as if a cloud had crossed over the room. "Yes, for a time we were close. But you must remember that Laura was twelve-and-a-half-years older than I. We never attended the same schools or had the same friends. She was the talented one, with her painting and her music. I was the adventurous one who was too often in trouble of one sort or another. As adults we were still opposites. Laura was married once, widowed young and never remarried. I've had four husbands and I'm contemplating a fifth. So you see, we were never alike, your mother and I. We never understood each other."

"But I remember what fun you two used to have."

"Yes, we did, when you and Carmen were little girls. When Carmen was born, Laura adored her so. It was then that we began to see each other often. She wanted a daughter so badly, but she was already in her forties...." Hester picked up a plate of lemon cookies and offered one to Adrienne. Adrienne shook her head, smiling, remembering those same round lemon cookies and how she'd never liked them.

Hester continued. "Two years after Carmen was born, Laura found you. It didn't surprise me awfully. When Laura wanted something badly enough, she managed to find a way to get it."

"And she never told you where she found me?"

"She never told anyone, but it was assumed that she found you on one of her trips abroad. After Geoffrey died, Laura traveled a great deal. Traveling seemed to be her way of coping with his death."

"I know she brought me back from one of her trips. I've seen photographs of the day we arrived home."

"Yes. Not long before that, she had returned from an extended trip, acting very restless and preoccupied, it seemed to me, though she denied anything was wrong. A short time later, perhaps two weeks, she left again without giving anyone any notice. No itinerary. Within days she was back, and you were with her. You were two, perhaps two-and-a-half."

"My birth certificate gives my birthplace as Suffolk County."

"I'm sure that certificate is bogus, just as these fortune-seeking riffraff claim. Laura brought you from overseas—I know it. But she would have needed the proper documents to get you into America. Were you able to find anything among your mother's papers?"

"Yes, old passports. I brought them." Adrienne reached into her handbag.

Hester studied the books in silence. Her gray hair was brushed back softly from her face, revealing the luster of pearl earrings. Adrienne could remember when Hester's hair was as black as Carmen's.

"Have you looked carefully at this picture, Adrienne? This baby looks a bit like you, but it isn't you. This passport is a deliberate forgery."

"To get me into the country."

"Yes. Laura may have stolen you, my dear. Why else would she need to falsify all these documents? Except...?"

"Except what, Aunt Hester?"

"Except that it would have taken so much longer to get you here legally. It may simply be that she was impatient. I do know this much. She wasn't certain of your age or your name, or anything else about you, so she couldn't ever have had your real birth certificate in her hands. She called you 'Adrienne.' Quite honestly, I argued with her about the name because I didn't think it suited you. You were such a delicate little child to be burdened with such a...a graceless sort of name. But Laura was absolutely set on it. The translation seemed to have significance for her."

Adrienne sat forward. "Translation? What does my name mean?"

"Your mother never told you? How odd. She mentioned it several times while I was trying to talk her into something more fittingly feminine."

"What does my name mean?" Adrienne repeated politely, trying to keep impatience from scratching her voice.

"It means, 'woman of the sea.' Which turned out to be quite ironic, because you were frightened to death of boats and oceans when you were little."

Rising from her chair, Adrienne began to pace while she stared at the passport photo of a baby. She turned back to the woman in raspberry silk. "Aunt Hester, there has to be someone who knows the truth about this! All these forgeries—someone obviously did them for mother."

"It was a long time ago, Adrienne. People die."

Adrienne sensed something in her aunt's hesitation, something guarded, untold. She came nearer. "Who? Who would have known? Please tell me!"

The older woman folded her slender hands in her lap and sighed. The way she blinked and glanced away reinforced Adrienne's suspicion that there was something more. Seconds lapsed into eternity while Hester gazed at a painting on the wall, a dark seascape done in oils, one of Laura Canaday's earlier works.

"Please tell me, Aunt Hester!"

The faded eyes moved back to Adrienne, filled with a strange sadness. "The only person I can think of who might have known was Raleigh Janssen, Carmen's father."

Adrienne drew a quick breath. "Carmen's father? Your...?"

"My third husband. Raleigh was Laura's attorney. They were very close friends. I think she may have confided in him."

"But Raleigh Janssen has been dead for years!"

"Eleven years. And we were divorced many years before that, so I don't have any of Raleigh's personal belongings. Carmen has them. She is his only child." Hester sat forward and poured tea into both cups very ceremoniously, needing, Adrienne sensed, something to do with her hands.

Setting down the china teapot, she continued . "It's extremely doubtful he'd have left any questionable records pertaining to Laura's affairs. Raleigh wouldn't have been that careless."

"But it can't be just a dead-end! There must be some way."

"My attorney suggested we hire a detective agency to retrace Laura's steps to see if we can find anyone else in her life at the time who might have helped her. We can do that, Adrienne."

She stopped pacing again and sat across from her aunt. "I have very little money now. Everything is frozen except my trust fund and—"

"Money is of no concern," Hester interrupted with a sweep of her hand.

"But suppose I lose everything and can't pay you back...for years?"

"You won't. No thief is going to take a penny of *my* niece's legacy." She hugged the younger woman. "I know you're disappointed that I couldn't tell you more, darling. I wish I could be of more help to you."

"Thank you for sticking by me," Adrienne whispered with misting eyes, embracing her aunt. "What would I do without you and Carmen?"

"We are a very small family, dear. But we are a strong family. Always remember that."

ADRIENNE SAT in jeans and a pink short-sleeved sweater at the edge of a pool at Pacific Laboratory for Cetacean Communications Studies, watching three bottle-nosed dolphins. One had been playing with a rubber basketball when she arrived. He continued pushing the ball about with his nose, but his poolmates were paying no attention to the game.

If she looked down the slope toward the ocean, she could see the large pool that housed Aphrodite and Ulysses. Kendall and Brian were working there again this afternoon. Ken's body was a blurred silhouette against the sun; Brian was probably at the computer. She could hear their voices on the still afternoon air — male voices mixed with soft calls of birds and splashing of the big silver animals in the pool beside her. When she lowered her hand into the water, one of the dolphins approached, brushing by her slowly. Like the others she had met this past week, this dolphin acted unusually friendly. She was immersed in a feeling of belonging here. Some part of her, certainly, belonged here. It made no sense, but she felt it, believed it. For some reason, she was drawn to this alien world like a pin to a magnet.

Ken was standing on a low platform, rising and bending, extending his hands in the air. She didn't dare approach that area as long as he was working. Aphrodite might decide to socialize again in the middle of everthing, and Ken would be angered by the interruption and then there would be no point at all in telling him she had come to ask a favor.

A young woman in the lab's main office had been cordial when she had asked if she could wait for Kendall Burke. So Adrienne had wandered about the grounds until she'd stumbled across this pool at the top of a hill. Just being near dolphins again lighted sparks of wonder inside her—luminous little spurts of joy, like phosphorescent sparkles on the sea at night. And time, caught in small breezes and bird songs and soft alien eyes that watched her, dissolved into silky waves of sadness and of joy, like the eternal moving of the tides. The dolphins were like warm memories blowing softly through the mind as they swam, touching things past, things out of reach, things she ought to know and didn't.

Sensing a human presence near, she turned.

He stood, barefoot, in swim trunks. His gray T-shirt was half wet and half dry. She had the feeling he had been watching her, because he didn't speak at once. Instead he sat down beside her at the pool's edge and mumbled, "I didn't expect to see you again."

She had forgotten the timbre of his voice and what that voice could do to her equilibrium. It was too soon to take on the challenge of his eyes, so she kept her gaze on the pool, where the playful dolphin was refusing to share his rubber basketball. "I made certain I didn't interrupt your work this time."

"Did you come alone?"

She nodded. *No sense delaying*, she told herself. *Just blurt it out.* "I came to ask a favor."

"I was afraid of that," he muttered softly.

"Why 'afraid'? Do you never grant favors?"

"Sure, sometimes. You want me to explain the program of communication experiments we've set up?"

"No. I'm curious about your program, but this is something far more important to me. Something I feel I can't live without."

His dark-blue eyes narrowed into slits. She thought he started to say something that he thought better of. Then his eyes opened like little curtains on a puppet stage, revealing the same sparks of mischief she had seen on Sunday, when her soaked clothes had been clinging shockingly to her body.

"Do I have something you can't live without?"

Never say "can't," she scolded herself while adjusting the gauge of her temper tolerance up ten degrees to accommodate the man's attitude. She forced a smile. "Power, Mr. Burke. You have the power to smash the major fantasy of my life right into the rocks if you won't allow me to do it!"

One thick eyebrow raised. "I doubt any rational man would try to smash your fantasies, Adrienne."

She fell off guard. No, she was pushed off guard by a gentle murmur of her name. He remembered her name and said it as though he were used to saying it, as though he were used to thinking it! It sounded so incredible—the sound of her name on his lips. In her dream, when he said her name underwater, it had come out only bubbles.

She leaned slightly away from him in an act of self-preservation. "Then you won't say no?"

"That depends."

"On what?"

"On what the favor is. I could use more hints, since you seem to want to play games with me. Let's see. It's a major fantasy, something you can't live without, something you need me for. Hmm..." He rubbed his chin thoughtfully. "And it's something we don't do with clothes on, right?"

Adrienne flushed crimson. This man was accusing her of playing stupid games? Unless he really thought...no, he couldn't! Or could he? This was California, after all, where reputedly anything goes. Her eyes darted from his sensuous mouth to his chest, where muscles showed through the half-wet shirt. The even rise and fall of his breathing gave no hint of what was inside him—in his head or in his heart. He was so disgustingly calm and cool! Was she supposed to assume he was propositioned every day of his life? Well, fine. She could call his arrogant bluff.

She licked her lips. "That's right. I wouldn't do it with clothes on."

"And you need my cooperation."

"Definitely."

His feet were dangling in the water. He leaned forward, elbows on his knees, feigning deep thought as he watched the dolphins. She studied the back of his tanned, perspiring neck, below the line of curling dark hair.

After what seemed an eternity, he said, "I'm sorry. I'll have to say no."

"What?"

"We have a rule against letting people swim with the dolphins."

She was glad he wasn't looking at her, because red wasn't her best color. Her words came out half sputtered, half whispered. "So you knew the favor I wanted?"

"A lot of people ask it. We have no insurance to cover accidents."

The disappointment fell like a blanket over her, so heavy it almost crushed her anger with its weight.

"If you knew, why did you have to tease me?"

He had no answer. He was still looking at the dolphins and not at her.

"You were trying to scare me away, weren't you?"

He lowered his head slightly. She saw his shoulders heave in a small sigh.

"Why?"

In a voice so low she barely heard it, he said, "You don't scare easily, do you?"

"Of course not! But I'm not sure I can say the same about you. You haven't answered me. Why do you want to scare me away?"

After a long pause, he answered, "These dolphins are wild animals. You could get hurt."

"I wouldn't get hurt and you know it." She reached down to pet one of the dolphins who had come to the edge to socialize again. "Make an exception for me."

"I can't, Adrienne. If word ever got out that we let outsiders in the dolphin pools, we'd have so many people bugging us to do the same, we wouldn't get any work done. And I told you, we don't have insurance."

"If you keep mentioning risk, I swear I'll push you in the water."

He looked at her strangely. She thought for a second or two that he was about to smile, but the smile never blossomed. His eyes were impossible to read; they almost offered an apologetic admission that his lame excuses were ridiculous. Almost, but not quite. Again she visualized pushing Kendall Burke into the water, but realized it was doubtful he cared a whit whether he was wet or dry or even if he knew the difference.

She met his enigmatic eyes. "Dammit, Ken, it's terribly important to me!"

"Why?"

"I..." She had to grope for words; she had made the error of assuming he would automatically understand. "I...just have very strong feelings for the dolphins. It's hard to explain why the experience of swimming with them matters so much to me. It just does."

She had been gazing at the tight pull of his shirt across his shoulders and his back as he leaned forward, and she noticed the rise and fall of his breaths halt for some seconds, then accelerate raggedly. He said in a soft voice, "I'm sorry. Brian and I have strict rules. I can't allow it."

She sat in blank silence, just watching the slow circling of the dolphins. The cooing of a dove wafted above a small breeze that whispered through her hair. And his.

At length she stood up, her stomach knotted by this twist of disappointment. "I'm sorry, too. But I can respect the fact that you have rules." She ached to ask him if she could see Aphrodite again today or some other time, but knew that would just make the longing and the frustration worse.

Ken did not rise; he sat there like the statue of *The Thinker,* with his dark hair rippling in the breeze and his private thoughts hidden deeply within him. Why did she feel such pain at having to say goodbye to someone she never knew? Her stinging pride braced her and served to help steady her voice. "Well...goodbye, then."

His back straightened; he turned with a frown. "Adrienne, I..."

She forced a smile. "It's all right. It was brazen of me to ask—not the sort of thing I usually do."

She turned abruptly, sliding her sunglasses from their perch in her hair down over her eyes, which were smarting from sunlight on water or from flying specks of hurt or both.

Walking down the sloping path under moving shadows of trees, hearing the ocean in the distance, she longed for something familiar, longed for some comfort of her own world again: her music. She longed for her home, but her home was empty now. Longed for New York, but New York would not be the same without Richard. Still, her music was there....

Adrienne sighed. Her music wasn't in New York; it was with her—in her heart and her head and her hands. Only once or twice in her life had she been away from a piano for this long. Now, caught in a coil of loneliness, she longed for the comfort, the therapy, of her music. Perhaps Aunt Hester had a piano; she hadn't thought to ask.

The path led past the main building and to the parking lot beyond. Her pace quickened with a mounting desire just to be out of here. With shaking hands, she opened the door of Carmen's yellow Triumph. She was sliding behind the wheel, when the voice rose out of the silence she had left behind her.

"Adrienne, wait!"

She turned to see Kendall running barefoot down the path toward her. The turbulence trembled all through her. She clutched Carmen's keys tightly.

He leaned against the car and waited for his laboring breath to give his voice a chance. She said nothing, only waited, looking up at him, feeling vulnerable and confused. He seemed larger than before. Her heart was pounding as if she were the one who had been running.

"Brian and the others leave about five-thirty," he said, still sucking for breath. "It would have to be after that. We'll just not let anyone know."

The pounding in her breast increased to thundering. For a moment longer she stared up at him, trying to absorb what he had just said. "Are you sure?"

He smiled. "Did you bring a suit?"

"Sure. . .of course." He had actually smiled, and Carmen was right, she thought giddily and all out of context to the significance of the moment. When Kendall Burke smiled he was frighteningly near perfection—even closer than the nude marble statue of Hermes she had fallen in love with at the age of ten, in Athens. Hermes didn't smile; after all, certain vital parts of the statue were missing, broken off. Ken, who wore so little besides the rare smile, obviously had nothing missing. Incredible—a living man more perfect than Hermes! Adrienne scolded herself for her flying, erotic thoughts and decided that the excitement of Ken's change of heart had brought her dangerously close to hysterics. The news that she was going to actually have the chance to swim with dolphins was just more than she could handle so suddenly; she had only just fully registered Ken's refusal.

He looked at his watch. "It's just after four o'clock now. There's the Sea Cliff across the road. They have a quiet lounge there, if you don't mind waiting until around six."

"Certainly I don't mind waiting! Though I think it may be the longest two hours of my life."

He straightened, lifting his arm from the top of the car.

"Ken, how can I say how much I appreciate—"

He interrupted, with only a fraction of his smile remaining. "I'll see you later."

His exit was abrupt. Adrienne sensed he had serious doubts about what he had just done. But it didn't matter. He had done it!

SHE ENTERED a lobby of blue Spanish tiles and exotic potted greenery. A fountain splashed in the center under a skylight. To one side, in a dining room set with light-blue tablecloths and blue candles, two couples sat by windows with an ocean view. On her right, the lounge opened through a wide arch. This room, dominated by a grand piano, was arranged with comfortable chairs and love seats around small glass cocktail tables. A small mirrored bar was tucked into one corner. Plushly carpeted, lighted by chandeliers, the Sea Cliff lounge was tastefully elegant. Adrienne was greeted by a young man dressed in a Mexican embroidered blouse.

"I want a very light lunch," she told him, wondering if she would even be able to swallow, she was so excited. "But I'd like to make a phone call first."

The host directed her to a phone, with an invitation to sit anywhere she liked, either in the restaurant or the lounge. She left a message on Carmen's answering machine that she would be delayed, feeling guilty about keeping the car so long. But this was a once-in-a-lifetime emergency. A gin and tonic might calm her rising jitters, she decided, wishing Kendall had given her some hint as to why he had changed his mind. He hid his feelings very well and he was a man, Adrienne strongly suspected, who marched to his own drummer.

There were no other customers in the lounge this midafternoon. The bartender, drying glasses, smiled a greeting. Adrienne sat down in one of the black leather swivel chairs at the bar.

"What is the lady's pleasure?"

She ordered a seafood salad and the gin and tonic, and sat clicking her fingernails nervously against the bar top.

"In a hurry?" the bartender asked. He was a handsome man, quite overweight in a way that was almost becoming. He looked as if he might have been a pro-football lineman a few years and a few hundred beers ago.

"I'm in no hurry at all. In fact, I have nearly two hours to kill."

"Ah, I see. Waiting for someone."

"In a way." Her eyes scanned the dimly lit room and focused covetously on a magnificent black grand piano.

The bartender set a tall glass in front of her. "Do you play?"

"What?"

"The piano."

"How did you know?"

"You're looking at that Steinway the way a jewel collector looks at a rare emerald."

She sipped the cool drink and smiled.

"Since you have time to kill, why not play something?"

"What do you want to hear?"

The man thought for a moment, resting one elbow on the bar. "'Some Enchanted Evening.'"

Not his type of song at all, she thought, smiling, and went to the piano. She played a scale to test the touch, then offered her audience-of-one a medley of melodies from *South Pacific*. The music drew one of the couples from the dining room into the lounge. Two waiters in sequined Mexican vests materialized at the doorway and stood smiling with approval.

As soon as the medley was over, the couple requested "Behind Closed Doors." Adrienne was enjoying herself. She hadn't played popular music since the last big winter party in New York. But music always came back to her, the way the smell of lilacs came back in the spring as though it had never left.

A slim man in a white shirt and jeans leaned against the piano, watching her hands with deep concentration. She hadn't seen him come into the room or even felt his presence until he was already there, above her. Adrienne was uncomfortable with anyone that close when she played—a little self-conscious about the scars on her left hand and a little crowded for breathing space. She raised her light-blue eyes to meet the man's gray ones.

"Do you play Chopin?"

"Yes."

"Would you?"

Adrienne shrugged with a smile, loving the feel of this piano, loving the chance to play again, the chance to get back within herself, to feel the music again. She slid into Chopin's "Polonaise in A Flat," lightly at first, then losing herself, playing as though in spotlights to an audience of thousands.

Afterward, awe-filled silence fell over the room. Then applause.

The slim man with the gray eyes, staring, said, "You're major league! How come I don't know you?"

"I'm from Boston." Adrienne rose and returned to the bar where a waiter had just set down her lunch. The gray-eyed man sat beside her. "You played those people's request without any hesitation at all. Can you play any request?"

"I try."

"You've worked in lounges?"

"No. Countless parties, though. I'm pretty good at playing by ear."

"I've never heard anyone better."

She was stirring her drink. "Thanks."

"I'm Robert Gentry." He extended his hand and gave a bow of his head. "Owner and manager. I wish I could hire a pianist with half your style. In twelve years in this business I've never found anyone who could play Chopin the way you just did. You play concerts, I'll bet."

"Sometimes."

Robert Gentry ordered himself a Scotch and sat watching Adrienne in the mirror as she nibbled at the salad. She was aware of his eyes. She was also fighting a nervous twitching in her stomach, much like stage fright before a performance. The fluttery fluctuations of excitement and fear had been building ever since Ken's surprise reversal. It was almost impossible to eat.

The day had taken on a gauzy veil of unreality. Dolphins, Chopin, an almost deserted lounge on the sea coast, Ken waiting for her. Boston so far away, New York so far. Music at her fintertips, dolphins so close now. So close. And Ken waiting. She looked frequently at her watch.

"I'll give you a job here," Robert Gentry said suddenly. "Miss—"

She looked at him, startled. "Canaday. Adrienne Canaday."

"Miss Canaday, why not play here, if only for the summer season? Four, five nights a week, whichever you prefer. I'll pay a hundred dollars an hour in addition to tips. Consider it a temporary diversion, if you will. One can always find new adventure in diversions."

Adrienne could not help but note surprise on the bartender's face. He moved a short distance away and got busy wiping the counter.

"I'm not looking for a job, though," she said pleasantly.

Robert Gentry smiled. "I know. You're on vacation, right?"

"Yes."

"Well, one never knows. The offer stands. I'd rather listen to a good piano than make love. You see, I'm a simple man who has a passion for music."

She sat in silence, slowly sipping her drink. Now and then the handsome bartender would turn toward her, eyeing her curiously with a private smile.

"Even if you'd agree to play here just a few evenings while you're in town, I'd be truly honored," Gentry coaxed.

"I'll think about it."

The owner of the Sea Cliff sighed, obviously not satisfied, resting his chin in his palms so heavily that the corners of his mouth were turned up in a clownlike grin. He sat staring at his own glum image in the mirror. "I discover gold and it slides through my fingers like dust."

He refused to allow Adrienne to pay for her lunch.

SHE FOUND KEN WORKING with the computer equipment beside Aphrodite's pool, where they had first met. He directed her to a bathhouse in which she could change. The room was spacious and clean and painted white. There was one shower stall, a toilet stall and sink, and a small table, very stark, utilitarian, like everything at the lab. She wondered who else used this room; there were no clothes left here, nothing that might belong to Ken or Brian. The more she tried to hurry, the more things went wrong. She tripped over her jeans and fell with a thud against the wall. The snap on the neck of her sweater caught in her hair. And she found a hopeless knot in the string straps of her bikini top.

Why had she brought a bikini, anyhow? She should have contained her eagerness long enough to shop for a modest one-piece suit that was more appropriate for an occasion as significant as being invited into a pool full of dolphins. Something in a blue shimmery fabric would have been perfect. How the devil was a person supposed to untie a stubborn knot with such trembling fingers? Ken was going to wonder what was taking her so long in here; he wasn't the patient type. Becoming semihysterical with fear that the knot might be permanent, she twisted around, slamming the knot desperately against the sink.

Coming face to face with an image in the mirror that registered such classic panic, she had to stop and stare. Strained giggles surfaced and changed the face. She had obviously gone completely mad. Worrying about wearing the right outfit to impress dolphins, for heaven's sake! They wouldn't care—nor, for that matter, would Kendall Burke. Laughing at herself saved her, relaxed her enough to approach the knot more calmly and loosen it. She scolded herself for losing control. She would relax, stroll out calmly and find out which pool to jump into. Or should she dive in? The way her knees were buckling, she would be accomplishing an athletic feat just to lower herself over the side.

With a black-and-white striped towel thrown casually over one shoulder, she walked barefoot out toward Aphrodite's pool to look for Ken.

4

As ADRIENNE came around the corner of the bathhouse the huge male dolphin made a leap into the air, his silver sides gleaming, his flukes slapping hard, splashing noisily. Startled, she stepped back, amazed at the size of the animal.

"That's Ulysses's way of celebrating," she heard Ken call. "I told him you were coming in—sometime within the hour."

Of course a crack about how long she'd taken to change! Adrienne turned in the direction of his voice and blinked in surprise. Ken was in the pool! So he intended to participate in her fantasy. Or maybe he didn't trust Ulysses.

It was difficult to see Ken's eyes because he was looking into the setting sun, which was hanging over the ocean near the horizon. But it was not difficult for Adrienne to feel sparks flying from those alert eyes when she discarded the towel and walked in her black bikini to the pool edge. This attention caused Adrienne to become shivery and more aware of her body than she had ever been in her life. There was a tense, painfully long silence before he spoke again.

"I forgot to warn you. The water's cold."

Nervously she lowered herself into the pool, trying not to grimace at the shock. Aphrodite swam near with an eager greeting. The dolphin's approach was such a thrill that Adrienne forgot the water temperature immediately, and when she reached out, Aphrodite responded with a brush of her body against Adrienne's arm. Ken kept his distance, not interfering. Within minutes, Adrienne was stroking the dolphin's head.

It was so easy to forget reality in this surreal place. The haunting sensation of déjà vu was strong enough to overpower her for the first minutes with the dolphin. What puzzled and amazed her was the depth of love she felt for these strange, shapeless creatures. It surpassed all logic.

Ulysses floated nearby with some caution. He lay on the surface, watching Adrienne curiously and refusing to come any closer. She talked to him softly, offering friendship he would not accept. Aphrodite competed boldly for Adrienne's attention. They swam together—the woman and the dolphin—to the deep end of the pool and back, making little dives and circles.

So entranced by the electric harmony she found with the dolphins, Adrienne had, for a time, forgotten Ken. Squinting through a spray of water, she caught sight of him standing waist-deep toward the shallow end. She wondered how he could stand still in the cold water without freezing. She swam to him, and found that when she stood next to his six-foot frame, the water level reached her armpits. She was keenly aware of his eyes on her as she moved to shallower water.

Both dolphins hovered near them. One would circle away and jump around and then return.

Ken said, "I'm having a hard time believing what I'm witnessing, Adrienne. They are actually excited about your being here. I've never seen dolphins respond to a stranger quite like this. What do they know about you that I don't?"

She smiled, treading water just to keep warm. "Maybe it's true what you said—that they can read my feelings."

"What are your feelings?"

"It's awfully hard to put feelings into words. But here with the dolphins it's like...almost like a linking of souls...or...or like connecting to something lost and now found again." She was short of breath. "What do you think it means, Ken?"

"I don't know what it means," he answered softly. "You're not a mermaid, are you?"

"With the terror of water I used to have, I hardly think so."

"I don't see any signs of terror."

"I overcame it, but it took years."

A cloud of disbelief lingered in his eyes. The way he was looking at her was unnerving; Adrienne felt as if she had to keep treading water to stay buoyant and not sink under the weight of his stare. She didn't know enough about dolphins to understand why their reactions to her stunned him. But he *was* stunned. And he was curious.

She said, "Ulysses won't let me pet him."

"No one here has ever petted him. A few days after Ulysses was captured in Florida, he was enticed into a very small enclosure, where he was kept for hours before being loaded in a sling to be flown out here. It's hard to imagine what a small enclosure would feel like if you'd never known anything but open sea. They tell us Ulysses was friendly enough before, but he never got over being tricked. I think he was a leader of his clan in the wild. His actions make me think so."

Intelligent tursiops eyes held Adrienne spellbound. "Ken, I'll never be the same after this. It's as if...I know it sounds silly, but it's as if I wasn't complete before, as if this is something I was meant to do." The words were inadequate to explain the sensation of dolphins touching her under the water, for the sensation was both new and not new—like a living dream. She was shaken once again with the feeling that time somehow had outdistanced this day to place it in the wrong zone, making all of it unreal. And the day would be gone and never return, and when she looked back it still wouldn't be real. Today's moments would melt into her past, but their magic would never leave her.

They swam to the deeper end. Treading water, she smiled. "Maybe I was a dolphin in some past life."

"Who knows?" he smiled back, and then he drew near, so near she felt an entirely new bewildering sensation—that of his leg brushing hers. And not accidentally. The first touch of Ken's body to hers underwater was shockingly sensual. Arousal flared up in Adrienne—a desire so wild, so powerful, it weakened her body. She started to sink and caught herself, hoping he didn't notice that his gentle teasing was shock enough to threaten her with drowning. No man's nearness had ever been so threatening.

Their eyes met. Neither spoke. Ken's lips moved as if he were about to say something. But instead he allowed himself to be distracted by Aphrodite, who was heading toward them with a red rubber ball.

"Aphrodite wants to play," he said.

"Was the ball her idea, or did you signal her?"

"Her idea," he grunted, reaching up to catch the ball as the dolphin tossed it into the air. "My mind was elsewhere just now. Here, catch!"

"Wait!" she gurgled, with both hands extending toward him. When she missed the ball, sinking to her forehead, the dolphin charged forward to catch it.

"We'd better move to the shallow end before you drown," Ken decided.

She sidestroked to safer water. "How can you tread water without arms?"

"Practice." Ken caught the ball from Aphrodite again and threw it to Adrienne.

This time she caught it and tossed it to the dolphin. Ulysses stood by, overseeing the game like a parent watching young children play, too aloof to take part himself. Another side to Kendall was emerging—the playful side—with abandoned, spontaneous laughter whenever the dolphin's clever antics outshone the skill of the humans. It was clear he was not doing this grudgingly, as a favor, after all; he was enjoying himself.

The game lasted for more than fifteen minutes. Adrienne wondered, watching Ken, how often he allowed himself the luxury of play. Perhaps seldom, perhaps often; from what she knew of him, it was impossible to guess. So much about this man was impossible to guess. When he had touched her earlier, holding his leg against hers so that she knew it was deliberate—was he only teasing?

She began to tire. He must have noticed, because he panted, "Are you getting cold?"

"I'm beginning to."

"Ready to get out? It's almost too dark to see."

It was more request than question. And even though she hated to have this end, the water was quite cold and dusk was becoming night. He made no offer to turn on the lights over the pool.

Ken pulled himself out first and threw her towel to her. He had no towel and he didn't seem to mind, even in the chilly evening air. When she started toward the bathhouse to change, he went in the opposite direction without a word. She wondered if he would still be around when she came out. Probably. Someone had to lock up.

A few minutes later she emerged, dressed in her jeans and pink sweater, her short, towel-dried blond hair curling around her face. It was almost dark.

Kendall stepped out of the shadows, wearing jeans and a sweat shirt. "Would you like a beer? Or coffee?"

She had begun to shiver. "Coffee sounds wonderful."

He led her down the slope of path to the main building, and entered through a back door. They stood in a small studio apartment, a rather stark room painted beige and white. Dozens of photographs of dolphins and whales covered the walls. A table and chairs took up one side of the room, a couch and television set the other. A bookcase was overflowing with papers and books, and there were more papers and books piled on the table and on the couch.

Adrienne asked, "Do you live here?"

"Only during the week." He stepped behind a counter to the tiny galley kitchen. "I live at Shelter Island Marina on weekends, when my work schedule permits. Sit down, get comfortable. Just push that stuff out of your way. Is instant coffee okay?"

"Instant is fine." She gathered papers carefully, a collection of handwritten notes, and set them on the table. "Do you live on a boat?"

He nodded. "It's not a very classy boat, but it's adequate bachelor quarters."

She sat on the couch, which she supposed must also be a bed. None of the three doors leading from the room, all of which stood ajar, led to a bedroom. One door revealed a bathroom, another a closet and the third opened into, of all things, an indoor pool. She could see water in the thin spray of light from the doorway; otherwise the pool was dark. She noted, too, in her survey of Ken's temporary quarters, that at least half the cabinet doors hung open. Apparently the man had a problem closing doors.

From the couch that was also a bed she asked, "Is it a sailboat?"

He filled a tin pot from the tap and set it on the burner. "In a moment of madness I traded a good ketch for this cruiser. I regret it in a way, but I didn't have time for sailing anymore. And she does give me more living space."

He sat down on the opposite end of the couch and relaxed, ankle over knee. He was still barefoot. "Well, pretty lady, was swimming with dolphins what you expected?"

"It was more, Ken. It was like being privileged to enter another world. What must it be like to swim with them in open sea? Have you ever done that?"

"Very few people have ever done that. Some species—not tursiops—enjoy following ships, but they usually disappear if a diver goes into the ocean."

"Yet they're so social in captivity."

"They're social by nature. It's believed that when one is banished from its group it will die. A few in captivity have preferred to die rather than be isolated. Humans have destroyed too many of them one way or another through ignorance. One of our objectives here at the lab is to provide more information to oceanariums around the world by researching dolphins' social habits."

"I assumed captured dolphins were automatically tame."

"A few accept humans within minutes. Others become neurotic, even commit suicide. But most of those who are able to adjust seem fairly content. As content as we could expect prisoners to be. For reasons I don't understand, they don't try to escape back to the sea."

"Never?"

"Almost never. Once they're used to humans they tend to want human company. Of course, looking at it from their point of view, it's a big treacherous ocean out there and they may be terrified to be alone in it."

Adrienne was thoughtful, considering the wide, dark sea. "How could humans who have met dolphins not fall in love with them?"

"Are you talking about yourself?"

"It's a very powerful infatuation, Ken."

The same strange, curious expression she had seen in the pool passed over his face again. "I understand the infatuation. In your case it seems to be on both sides. If I didn't know better, I'd swear they knew you. Is there some secret between you and the dolphins?"

"'Secret'?" She smiled uneasily, because Ken hadn't said it jokingly; a rustle of distant thoughts edged his voice.

He rubbed the back of his neck. "I'm not sure what I just saw out there in the pool. Some kind of interspecies communication on a subliminal level is the only way I can explain it. How do you explain your fascination?"

"I can't. Oh, I always loved to read about dolphins, especially when I was a kid. I used to dream about them sometimes."

"You did? What sort of dreams?"

"Just. . .dolphins swimming in the ocean. In my dreams they were always friendly—like Aphrodite—and I could touch them."

"You seemed so eager to touch them now. That's a natural reaction with any animal encounter, of course. But the minute you did touch Aphrodite you forgot I was there. You seemed oblivious to everything else. And so did she." He rubbed his neck again. "Fascinating. . . ."

Gently, a little dreamily, he began tracing the lines of her scars, asking, with his fingertips, a silent question. She allowed the moments to pass in timid silence rather than try to explain that she had no idea what injury had caused those scars, or when. They had just always been there, for as long as she could remember.

From the stove the kettle was screaming. Ken released her hand with some reluctance and rose to make their coffee.

Adrienne was relieved the subject of the scars was closed. He had asked without asking and received no answer; she doubted he would ask again.

When he set the coffee mugs on the small table by the couch, steam rose into the light of the lamp like mist to sunlight. Sitting down closer to her this time, running his fingers through his thick brown hair, he said, "We're a total mismatch, you and I."

"Are we? I hadn't noticed."

He smiled. "A lovely lady like you, polished to a sheen with culture and high breeding, must have noticed you're in the company of a guy who is less than half civilized."

She shook her head. "You're the rugged outdoors type, perhaps, but I'd stop short of calling you 'Tarzan.'" She took a slow sip from the coffee mug and chuckled. "Although I'll have to admit you and Tarzan sometimes dress alike."

"We probably have similar grooming habits, too. I could lose my comb and not know it was lost for two days, what with being in and out of water all day long. Still, I was so set on impressing you that I found my comb tonight, which proves you are a threat to the fundamental structure of my life-style. A threat..." he repeated in a husky whisper, brushing her forearm gently with his fingers.

This comment would take some concentrated analysis, but it was hard for Adrienne to analyze anything when Ken was so close and his voice so velvety. Was he admitting he worried about being vulnerable to her charm? Or was he saying he resented her "high breeding"?

So graceful and subtle were his moves that before she realized he had shifted his position on the sofa, she felt his arm around her. He bent toward her and kissed her forehead gently, then her lips.

Adrienne's breath left her, but Ken's lips did not; their soft pressure increased on hers, until she began to experience a floating sensation. For one brief moment, she determined that she had to stay on the ground—she really had to. But then she couldn't think why staying on the ground mattered. So she felt for his wide, hard shoulders and pulled herself to him, returning the kiss, becoming lost in it. Finally he pulled away reluctantly and looked at her with eyes she could not read. Curiosity was there, and something more. Something primitive wakening! Some glint of wonder. Even some hint of regret.

He rasped, "I wasn't sure you wouldn't be insulted if I kissed you."

Adrienne's eyes grew wide. "'Insulted'?"

He smiled a slow, crooked smile. "I perceived a certain aloofness about you the day we met. This afternoon I thought you were being friendly because you wanted a favor. But in the pool you were different. You're different now."

"You're different, too. You're not angry or on the defensive about anything for a change. I thought you were the unapproachable one."

"I suppose I can be starchy, Adrienne. Brian assures me my social polish is badly tarnished."

"Well," she admitted, snuggling deeper into the cushions of the sofa. "Actually, you're not the first person who has accused me of acting aloof. I don't mean to be. It's shyness." An image kept intruding into the forefront of her mind—him sleeping here on this sofa. Right here, in this quiet room. His tanned skin would look very dark against white sheets, and he would sleep nude, of course, like Tarzan, his fingers curled, his eyes closed to all kaleidoscopes of the outer world and shadows of his eyelashes in the moonlight from the window...

His arm tightened around her, pulling her back to the moment. "You're a beautiful and mysterious woman."

He might have chosen other words if he had seen the picture in her mind just now, she thought recklessly as his head lowered to her again. His kiss came more slowly, more softly. And this time it was not the kiss of a stranger.

Summer storms were not strangers, either. Yet they crashed down to make the world tremble, just the same way. Slashes of fire across the sky. Wind gusting with loud whispers, threatening one's balance with its untamed power. His kiss was an electric storm with enough power to lure her from the safely defined senses of her everyday world. Never had she known such a kiss! It was ice and fire, lightning and rain, flesh and spirit all flashing together, leaving her filled with wonder.

And afterward, searching for his breath, Ken whispered, "How long will you be here?"

"Be where?"

"In California. Your cousin said you were visiting."

"I'm not sure. I may stay longer than I planned."

Her answer caused a strange, unsettled look to cross his eyes. "Because of the dolphins?"

"Partly."

He twisted a curl of her hair gently and looked into her eyes. "Are you running from something, Adrienne?"

She squirmed to put space between them, but it turned out to be less than an inch difference. "No...why?"

"Sometimes there's a look in your eyes of someone..." He hesitated, searching for a word. "Someone lost, perhaps. Or someone with problems."

She answered with a mellow smile, wanting to make light of this channel of truth he had just set to rippling. "My mother died suddenly three weeks ago. I'm still not used to the idea that she's gone. But adjusting seems easier here in California, where everything is new and unfamiliar. I need to let all the old places and memories gather dust for a while. I'm not eager to go home again."

"Then don't. Do you have to?"

"Not right away, I guess."

Ken fell into silence. He was still holding her, but he moved away now and reached for his coffee cup, and Adrienne saw that his hand was trembling. He hunched forward, leaning his elbows on his knees, holding the cup with both hands, deliberately distancing himself from her. "I had no right to kiss you."

No right? What did he mean, "no right"? She summoned the courage to ask, "Why not? Is there someone else who wouldn't think you had a right to kiss me?"

"What do you mean?"

"What do *you* mean?"

He shrugged helplessly. "You looked so lovely in the pool. You look so lovely now, and I let myself get carried away, that's all."

"That's all?" She lowered her eyes so he wouldn't see the hurt in them.

He did not look at her.

"You're trying to scare me away again," she said softly.

"And my next line is, as I recall, 'You don't scare easily.'"

"Your tactics are very devious...your reasons obscure. I assume you do have reasons."

"Yes," he admitted in an apologetic voice.

"Then you shouldn't have kissed me."

"Yes...no! Dammit, Adrienne, I don't know!" He turned to face her, his eyes sad and mysterious and very blue. "I wanted to kiss you, feel your body close to me. You do crazy things to me. I can't think rationally."

"Worse things have happened to people." Worse things were happening to her as they spoke. She wanted more than just his kiss and the feel of his arms and chest against her. This would never do! If she didn't get out of here, she would find herself doing something irreversible, such as trying to convince this incredibly handsome stranger that rational thinking was life's number one bore. He was trying hard to resist her, either out of respect for her, or for some other reason he had no intention of divulging. She knew it was difficult for him, because his voice was as shaky as his hands and he refused to look directly into her eyes. Who was he trying to protect—himself or her? And from what?

Confused and a bit frightened by her own unballasted feelings for him, Adrienne glanced at her watch. "I may be exiled from California sooner than I think if Carmen wanted her car tonight. I think I'd better go." Her voice was high and flat, and seemed to hang awkwardly in the air.

Ken rose to his feet when she did, pulling down the sweat shirt that had ridden up his back when he was shifting around on the couch.

"Thank you for an experience I'll never forget."

He grinned. "I hope you won't forget your swim with the dolphins, either."

She shook her head, laughing. "No, I won't forget the dolphins...either."

His large hand came to rest on her shoulder. "I'll walk you to your car."

The path was not well-lit; there were only small ground lights placed here and there. Ken walked with his arm around her. The closeness of his body was oddly satisfying. She longed for him to say, "Come on out again," or, "Could I call you?" or even a simple, "I'll see you." But he said nothing when she left except goodbye.

During the drive back to Pacific Beach, Kendall Burke's goodbye echoed in her whirling brain. The scent of his freshly showered skin was still with her. The strong press of his lips lingered on hers like fine brandy.

Was she crazy? It had been the company of the dolphins she had sought! And they, too, kept swimming through her thoughts: their smiles, their strange and friendly eyes glinting mysteries just out of reach. She had just had the experience of a lifetime with the dolphins! And yet Ken's voice still echoed, his kiss still burned.

New York and home were far, too far away. Warmth was here. Even music was here—the magnificent grand piano at the Sea Cliff. She had not found what she came to find in California, but there was so much else here that was bidding her stay: the dolphins' eyes, Ken's eyes, Carmen's laughter, the sun...even the music.

Adrienne's heart began to pound with the mercurial draw of a decision more impulsive than any she had ever made. "No, Ken," she said aloud in the dark of a California night. "No, I don't scare easily."

HE STOOD FOR A FULL MINUTE in the parking lot after Adrienne pulled out. Then, hands in his jeans pockets, still barefoot, he walked through the night shadows— back past the orca pool under construction, past two small training pools, just walking, gulping the night air, thinking. What was it that made him crazy around this woman? *Lust or fear—take your pick,* he scolded himself bitterly. *Take both, then. Dammit, take neither!*

She reminded him of a face on a magazine cover, a little too beautiful to be real. Under that surface was something vincible and well guarded. He felt she was running from something, whether she was willing to admit it to him or not. She had materialized too suddenly into his life, with her absorbing fascination for the dolphins and theirs for her.

It was baffling. His own experience with dolphins was only partly scientific. The other part was emotional. Admittedly, he'd always had a problem completely separating the two. Now he was no longer convinced that in communication studies, the two could, or even should, be separated. Adrienne had just demonstrated the power of emotion in communication. Ken was deeply moved by what he had seen. And he wanted answers—answers he feared he'd never find.

For all her claims of innocence, Adrienne was a mysterious and remarkable woman. Could her abrupt entry into his life have been only accidental? But of course it was accidental! And fleeting. He was sure he shouldn't have let his guard down and kissed her, though; that only made it worse. There was no denying the bewildering, overpowering compulsion they had both felt to be close and closer. And because she wanted it, too, that made it twice as hard to quarantine his own passion.

He demanded himself, in the slow coming down of the ocean night, to let it go. Adrienne Canaday was from another world, his opposite in every possible way. She was the worst thing that could happen to him. His work was too important and too threatened by a shutdown right now for him to get distracted by a woman. Especially not this woman.

5

"YOU'RE GOING TO *WHAT*?" Carmen raised her arms high
in the air.

They sat in the sunny kitchen of the Pacific Beach
apartment, Carmen in a sweat shirt and briefs, Adrienne in a short blue satin robe trimmed in lace.

"Why not, Carmen? I can certainly use the money
right now. I'm not ready to go home to mother's empty
house or to New York and all the friends I shared with
Richard. And I haven't done what I came here to do. I
haven't come any closer to discovering my roots."

The aroma of freshly brewed coffee filled the room.
Carmen poured milk and sugar into her steaming cup.
"Well, of course I want you to stay in San Diego. It's just
that I can't imagine you working in a bar! What would
your mother say if she were here.?"

"It's not a bar. It's a very elegant lounge. And it's only
temporary. A perfect solution for this unrest I'm feeling. I plan to lease a car today, and if you still want a
roommate, I'll pick up half the expenses on the
apartment."

Carmen let out an excited whoop. "Well, when you
put it that way, it sounds great! Oh, I knew you'd love
it here!" She began to beat out a rhythm on the table
with her palms, then paused suddenly and looked up.
"What really made you decide to stay, cuz? Does it have

something to do with Kendall Burke? Not that anyone would blame you! No one could be purely objective about that hunk. Imagine getting lucky enough to have a romp in his tank!"

"It isn't his tank, exactly. It belongs to Aphrodite and Ulysses. And the dolphins are part of the reason I want to stay here longer, Carmen. There's so much I want to learn about them."

"How much did you learn about their famous trainer?"

"About his personal life? Nothing. We discussed only dolphins."

"And then, after the pool adventure, you decided to accept this Mr. Gentry's job offer? Are you sure about it, cuz?"

"I'm going to be making music, which isn't even work for me, and I'll make good money for doing something I enjoy. When you see the place, you'll feel all right about it. Have Scotty bring you out."

Carmen didn't seem convinced. "How convenient that the Sea Cliff is right across the road from Ken's lab!"

"Yes, isn't it? I'll admit I like that part."

Carmen's dark eyes were shining. Outside, palm branches brushed the window of the third-story apartment. "Well, let's not tell my mother right away. She gets weak over shocks—such as her only niece working in a public lounge, for instance. Mother may have a couple of fainting spells over this."

Adrienne leaned over the table conspiratorially. "Carmen, did you know your dad and my mother were friends? He was her attorney, and therefore he was in a position to know—and to guard—her private affairs.

Hester told me Raleigh may have been the person who helped Laura smuggle me into America. Someone helped her get those false documents."

"Yeah, I know. Mom told me about it yesterday. I have trunks of my dad's things, all in the attic at mother's house. It's a shot in the dark, but any shot is worth a try."

"That's how I feel, even though mother's path seems to be well covered."

"Still, we may dig up something. Forty percent of all adoptees who search for their parents eventually find them. Something will break. Mother is going to hire a detective agency in Boston."

Adrienne sighed deeply. "You know, it's funny, Carmen. When I was with Ken Burke and the dolphins I forgot all about this family mess for a while. And afterward I caught myself thinking, what does it matter where I came from, anyhow, as long as I can live the way I want now? But the curiosity always takes over again and the ache to know comes back."

Carmen scowled. "All the secrecy...are you sure you really want to know what's behind it?"

"Yes, I want to know. I have to know." Adrienne glanced at the wall clock. "I think I'd better move if I'm going to lease myself a car today and buy a suitably daring gown—something smothered in black sequins. I told Robert Gentry I'd start my job tonight."

IT WAS A LONG WEEK for Adrienne, because she didn't hear a word from Ken. She thought of him each evening as she drove to the Sea Cliff, thought of how near he was—just across a tree-lined road, perhaps working late, or in the tiny apartment on the sofa that was also his bed. She wondered if there was another woman with him at night. He hadn't asked for her phone number when they'd said goodbye, so it was obvious he had no intention of calling her or seeing her again. And yet the way he had kissed her had been astounding—with his quickly caught breaths and the hot drumming in his chest. Thinking of him being over there, so close, was too easy, and too excruciating.

The dolphins had become a secret part of her, like the treasured memory of a summer love. She longed to see them, to be with them, but she couldn't impose on Ken. He had said goodbye as if that evening had been a sweet and passing thing and nothing more. Evidently it was nothing more—to him.

THE FOLLOWING FRIDAY NIGHT, Carmen and her boyfriend, Scotty Gilgood, drove out to the Sea Cliff to hear Adrienne play. They perched on bar chairs early in the evening, laughing with other customers, one of whom was Brian Palmer.

When Adrienne took her place at the piano and began to play, Brian, in jeans, sneakers and a red T-shirt, smiled and approached her, drink in hand. "If I'd known this place had gone first-class I'd have dressed for the occasion! I've been talking to your cousin. Couldn't believe it when she told me you're playing here now." He sipped from his glass. "I have to say you look different in this setting. Dry and sparkling!"

She smiled. "You make me sound like a glass of ginger ale."

"No, champagne." Brian leaned on the piano, adjusting his glasses. "How do you talk and play at the same time, Adrienne?"

"I don't pay much attention to what I'm saying."

He shifted and chuckled. "Dolphins like music. I think they prefer classical."

"I'm not surprised. Even plants prefer classical music."

"Yeah? I'll be damned! No wonder my spider plant is so vicious. It hates my jazz tapes!"

Brian's eyes shifted toward the door of the lounge. He straightened. "Well, well, here comes the rest of the cast. We have a tradition of Friday-evening happy hours over here, but usually Ken won't tear himself away from work to join us. Tonight we're highly privileged!"

Adrienne's back was to the door. She couldn't turn around. But even without looking up from the piano, she knew the exact moment Kendall Burke saw her.

BLACK SEQUINS SPARKLED under the chandelier. Short blond hair framed her face in wisps of gold. The shimmering dress, tightly fitted in the bodice, accenting the lines of her breasts, was high at the throat and long sleeved. Diamond earrings caught small fires of light when she moved.

Ken's tall, muscular form was locked in the archway like a statue while he gazed, awestruck, at the pianist. The young, red-haired woman with him tugged impatiently at his blue polo shirt.

When Brian waved a salute, Adrienne turned. Her eyes caught Ken's stare. He blinked. Like silver gift wrap, her smile unfolded from the sparkling shadows. His questioning eyes and his pale smile remained settled on her as he followed the young woman to a table across the room.

Adrienne could see him being drawn halfheartedly into conversation, ordering drinks and talking with Brian, who had found his way quickly to Ken's table. She wondered who the young woman was. Like Brian, Ken and the woman were wearing jeans. Tarzan in sneakers in a candlelit lounge. Friday happy hour. Brian was dominating the conversation, and Ken kept glancing toward the piano with the expression of someone looking at a ghost.

Flustered, Adrienne forced her attention to the music until she had finished the set. She was making her way across the room during the break, heading for the table Carmen and Scotty now occupied, when a large dark presence loomed in front of her. She looked up into Ken's deep-blue eyes.

For a time he only stood there, blocking her, his legs apart, his hands in his pockets. Finally he spoke, only the hint of a smile on his face. "Tourists from Boston can turn up in the strangest places." The voice was so deep its velvet sound hung in the smoke-filled air.

"It's been days since I was a tourist from Boston. I live in San Diego now."

He made no attempt to hide his surprise. "Was it anything I said?"

She looked up at him uncertainly. "How could it have been anything you said? You didn't say anything."

"Sure, I did. I asked if you were staying."

"Robert Gentry offered me this job the afternoon I was waiting for you. On the way home from the lab that night I decided to accept. It's only temporary."

He shook his head, bewildered. "I once told you, back in the days when you were a tourist, that I find you beautiful and mysterious. What an understatement, Adrienne, compared to the way I see you tonight! I could barely carry on an intelligent conversation at the table because I couldn't keep from staring at you in that gown and listening to you play. You're damned good. You aren't even using music!"

"It's not all that mysterious. Music is my second language. I'm working toward a graduate degree in piano."

"You see, lovely lady, how little I know about you? You drop such gems to me like cheese crumbs to a mouse."

"Oh. And what gems of information about yourself have you offered me?"

"No glittering gems here. I'm a primitive. My life story can be told in one word."

"Of course—dolphins." Adrienne wished to challenge this oversimplification, but it was the wrong time and place.

He lowered his voice. "When you go back to breathe life into that piano again, will you play something special for me?"

"With pleasure. What do you want to hear?"

"You decide." He winked and stepped out of her way.

She watched him cross the room in easy strides that were as uncommonly sensual as everything else about Ken Burke.

Fifteen minutes later, after half a glass of sherry with Carmen and Scotty, Adrienne returned to the piano. She felt the penetration of Ken's eyes and glanced in his direction to let him know she was ready to honor his request. The woman beside him was deep in conversation with Brian when Adrienne began to play.

He knew the song, all right. A look of mischief crossed his handsome face as he mouthed the words. "Send in the Clowns." Smiling, he raised his glass to her.

Ken didn't stay at the Sea Cliff much longer, although Adrienne didn't see him leave. The redhead who had come in with him remained in the lounge with Brian. Before the evening was over they had joined Carmen and Scotty. The liquor was flowing very freely at that table.

Carmen approached the piano once, quite unsteady on her feet. "Who'd have thought it would ever have come to this, cuz? When you had to practice two hours a day in your mother's music room and I used to wait on the steps playing paper dolls, who'd have thought you'd ever get this good? Only point one-seven-two pianists in fifty thousand ever get this damn good!"

Adrienne had been playing Tchaikovsky's Concerto No. 1 in B-Flat Minor, a request of Robert Gentry's. She was continuing with soft variations on familiar melodies from the classics, aware that few people here, except Mr. Gentry, were listening to the music at this late hour. "Carmen," she whispered, "you're totally smashed."

"We all are. Except Ken. Where is Ken, anyway?"

"He left a while ago."

"What a party pooper! Did he leave alone?"

"I wouldn't know."

Carmen grinned, balancing herself against the piano. "Did you see the look on his gorgeous face when he saw you tonight? I swear everybody saw it! Even Brian made a remark." She giggled. "Brian is so cute. It's a good thing for Scotty that I don't go for older men. Look at those two over there! Pals forever! The girl's nice, too. Her name is Melanie and she works at the lab. I said I'd figured she was Ken's date. She and Brian thought that was a great joke, but they didn't let me in on it."

Adrienne glanced at her watch. "I'm getting ready to wrap it up here. Why don't you and Scotty order some coffee before you drive home?"

"Good idea! We'll do that. Darn that Ken! Leaves just at the height of the fun. Where would he go at this hour?"

Adrienne sighed, picturing a yacht harbor, silent and dark in the dead of night.

THE FOLLOWING AFTERNOON, while Carmen was still in bed recovering, Adrienne drove to the Sea Cliff early to give herself a few hours to practice. The lounge was deserted when she sat down at the piano. Except for the bartender and Robert Gentry, who wandered in once and sat for half an hour without moving, there was no one to distract her during the entire afternoon.

Music was like the ocean. When she entered into it, it rolled over her and wrapped itself around her and became her. So it had been now with Rachmaninoff's Piano Concerto No. 2. She had brought the music to its dramatic finale when she looked up to see Ken leaning in the archway in faded jeans, his arms folded in front of him.

The arms unfolded slowly. He applauded as he pushed away from the wall. "I phoned over here to find out if you were working tonight, and they told me you were already here, practicing. I couldn't believe that was you I heard in the entrance. I thought I'd walked into a concert hall." He ran his fingers slowly through his thick brown hair. "Classical! Everything about you is classical."

Smiling light-blue eyes met his. "I'm sure you didn't come over here to tell me that."

"I came to tell you we had a birth at the lab the day before yesterday. I thought you might like to see a newborn tursiops."

A fresh, childlike excitement raced through her. "Yes, I would! When?"

"Now."

Heart pounding, she closed up her music and hurried across the room. No sparkling gown now. She wore crisp white slacks, high-heeled sandals and a blue-and-white-striped shirt. He smiled his crooked smile and surprised her by taking her hand.

Ten minutes later they were standing beside the indoor pool in the main building of the lab, watching the graceful circling of the mother tursiops with her baby at her side.

"We were lucky to get video tapes of the birth," Ken told her. "Dolphins are born tail first. The mother pushes the baby to the surface for its first breath. They must surface for every breath. Breathing's not an unconscious function as it is with us."

Spellbound, Adrienne watched the synchronous circling. Each time the mother rose for a breath, the baby at her side would do the same. Every few minutes, when the baby would drop back to nurse, its mother would squirt thick milk from her mammary glands into the little mouth.

She asked, "Is it a male or female?"

"We don't know yet. The sex organs aren't visible, and it will be several more days before I'll attempt to touch the baby."

The excitement rendered her giddy—a little dreamy. "Oh, Ken, you're so lucky to live with dolphins! Look, you can step right from your apartment to this pool! How I envy what you do!"

He smiled. "Most people don't see spending your life in water and in debt as a very enviable situation."

"Most people haven't experienced dolphins." She turned to look at his eyes, attempting to determine the depth of today's friendliness and his joy in sharing the excitement of the dolphin's birth.

The silence was broken by the sound of women's voices and seconds later Melanie Stevens entered the lab. She was followed by a young woman with a baby in her arms, a child of six or seven months, dressed in jeans and a tiny UCLA sweat shirt.

Melanie smiled a greeting at Adrienne as she said, "Ken, Betty Summers has brought Kevin out today. I told her I thought it would be all right."

"I know I was supposed to wait until tomorrow," the pretty brunette said with a self-conscious smile, balancing the baby on her hip and hurrying past Ken and Adrienne to the poolside. "But I was too excited to wait. Oh! What an adorable baby! Oh, he's gorgeous, Kendall! Is it a male?"

"We don't know."

"He's just lovely! Was it all right to bring Kevin today?"

"Sure," Ken said with a smile. "Why not?"

The woman set the child down, knelt beside him and began hurriedly undressing him.

Adrienne's curiosity lifted and skidded over the whole of this excursive scene. The unmarked margins of Ken's social behavior were a bit puzzling to try to decipher, as his usual lukewarm reception to intruders gave way to amicability, even warmth.

Betty chattered constantly to her son. "Oh, Kevie, do you see the little dolphin? Shall we say hello to the new little dolphin?"

Adrienne thought such a young baby couldn't understand much of what his mother was saying to him. Yet the boy demonstrated his enchantment of the water and the dolphins by squirming around and squealing.

Ken made introductions and some hurried explanations to Adrienne. "Betty is one of our three volunteers in an experiment to bring human and dolphin babies together. We want to discover whether any form of interspecies language develops between the babies as they become acquainted and grow accustomed to being together on a daily basis."

"Isn't it exciting?" The woman, still on her knees, beamed at Adrienne. "Kevin was born in water—a wonderfully successful birth—and he's been in water every day of his life."

"The kid's a strong swimmer, if you can fathom that, Adrienne," Ken said. "I couldn't believe it when I saw him swim the other day. Seven months old." He rubbed his chin thoughtfully and a frown creased his forehead. "Betty, I'm still worried about the temperature of the water. I want to get Kev measured for a little wet suit before we let him spend very much time in the pool. It's as warm now as we dare let it get. Today will have to be a really brief encounter, okay?"

Beside the naked child, the young woman was stripping down to a black one-piece swimsuit. "Okay. And I promise, we won't try to approach the dolphins. We'll just be in there so Kevin and the dolphin baby can see each other. I wouldn't want to upset the mother. We won't, will we?"

"Not if you don't approach them. I'd stay right by the edge, though, this first time, so they'll realize you're just observers." Ken moved to the pool rim, indicating he would be right there in case of anything unexpected.

Melanie had been standing a short distance away with her arms full of towels. She, too, came close to the edge now, as Betty, with the child in her arms, began to lower herself down a narrow ladder, letting out a cheerful shriek at the first shock of cold.

"Are you going in, Ken?" Melanie asked.

"No. This is just for mothers and babies."

At his first feel of water, the child squeaked with delight and began to swim, flailing his little arms and legs about on the surface of the water.

"Look at that! Kevin thinks he's a fish!" Melanie exclaimed.

From the moment the infant touched the water, Adrienne ceased to hear the voices of the adults. She had drawn in her breath as though she herself were entering the pool. Shivering, she felt the cold seawater draw itself around and hold her, numbing her with fear. Then every muscle in her body strained against the urge to rush toward the baby and pluck him from the water and into the safety of her own arms. Yet she couldn't move. A terror, crossing the gulf of years since her own childhood—the old, hideous terror—raced back to entrap her, paralyzing her.

Wizened moments of agony passed. Each time the small yawns of water swelled about the baby's face, Adrienne held her breath. For a time Ken and Melanie and Betty Summers were forgotten; even the dolphins were forgotten. Reality was trimmed to the circle of water holding claim to that baby's life. The pool had become the deep-bosomed ocean; she felt its rising and falling surface, heard its rhythmic, rasping breaths as it moved around and beneath the child.

With a start, Adrienne's consciousness spun out over the water to the circling dolphins, who swung suddenly very near the humans, the mother tursiops staying protectively on the outside. The little boy, kicking his legs, reached out toward the passing animals, almost touching the flukes of the mother. And as he did so, the dolphin slowed, floating on the surface for some seconds.

This simple, slowing motion—this motion of trust—seemed to throw a beam on Adrienne's blind, dark fear and lighten it. In that moment she knew for certain there was no threat to the baby. The child was safe.

Adrienne's heart was pounding. She felt faint.

"Adrienne!" Ken's voice coughed at her. "What's the matter?"

She struggled to return to the reality of the cold, gray pool and the humid air and Ken beside her. Tears were blurring her vision and streaking her pale cheeks. Gradually she came to realize she was grasping Ken's arm in a desperate grip; her nails were digging into his skin.

Through the glaze of tears, she stared dumbly at him.

"What's wrong? You cried out, Adrienne! Why are you crying?" His hand folded over hers, sending its warmth and strength to her.

"I...I don't...I don't know, Ken! The baby in the water...frightened me."

"Kevin is perfectly safe. You know he's perfectly safe in there."

"I...yes...of course I know it. I was just..." She brushed awkwardly at the tears on her cheeks. "I didn't know I cried out...I didn't mean to."

She was fighting her way back to the vivid living colors of reality, but the scallops of little waves on the pool's sides tended to hypnotize her; the silver-gray spinning dolphins swinging up to the water's surface, easing closer and closer to the human baby, left her spellbound. She was trembling with inexplicable feelings of joy and sadness. They were such powerful and profound emotions, so abruptly uncloaked, that she couldn't grasp their meanings.

A drop of blood appeared on Ken's forearm where her nails had clawed at him. Adrienne brushed at the scratch, then took another quick swipe at her wet cheeks and turned away from him, muttering an embarrassed apology. She felt his eyes on her, puzzled and concerned. He hadn't pulled his arm away when her nails had bit into his flesh, even though it must have hurt.

To her relief, Betty Summers was climbing out of the pool with her son. They had been too excited over the dolphins to notice Adrienne's tears. If they had heard her cry out, as Ken said she had, they gave no indication of it.

Betty wrapped her baby in an enormous white towel and pulled another around her own shoulders. "It's cold, Kendall! I think you're right about the wet suit." She rubbed vigorously, drying Kevin's shivering little body, while the boy's bright eyes remained fixed on the big sea animals. "Did you see it? The dolphin mother ignored us at first. Then she got curious and came right to us! She almost let Kevin touch her! This is going to be fascinating, just fascinating! Is the baby healthy, Kendall?"

"As far as I can tell it looks and acts fine. The mother—we call her 'Jillie'—is taking her maternal responsibilities very seriously. Sometimes with dolphins raised in captivity, we can't be certain they'll know enough about motherhood—they haven't had the proper chance to learn from their peers."

"Jillie's beautiful!" Betty snuggled down inside the towel and shivered. "Hey, maybe I need a wet suit myself for this water."

"I'd consider it. No point in being miserable if you're going to be here every day. Once we move the dolphins to the big pool, the water will be even colder."

When Betty and Kevin Summers and Melanie had gone, Adrienne examined Ken's wounded arm more carefully. "I'm sorry I did this to you. I guess I was so caught up in what was happening, I didn't realize...Does it hurt?"

"It's okay. I keep my tetanus shots up-to-date." His lips were smiling, but his blue eyes were not. "What upset you so much, Adrienne?"

"I wish I could answer you honestly—or even dishonestly, for that matter. I don't know what upset me. It was seeing the baby in the water...and the dolphins there with him. It was just...very emotional...I didn't mean to dig my nails into your arm."

"You were crying, too."

"That's...I guess I...thought he was in danger, Ken. He's so tiny to be in water so deep."

She felt a strong, male arm around her shoulders. "It was emotional for me, too, to see that encounter. But it was a far more emotional experience watching the tursiop's birth" Ken didn't press for a more logical answer to her tears, but the protection he offered with his silence failed to mask the disquiet in his eyes.

"I'm becoming more and more intrigued by your experiments in communication," Adrienne said, enjoying the warmth of his body next to hers. "Does this experiment with children have anything to do with your computer language research?"

"No, not a thing."

"Would you explain to me what you do with the computers?"

"Sure, if you have the time."

She nodded. He led her outside to the training pool, where computer equipment was set up behind glass screens for protection from salt spray. Brian Palmer was there, leaning over a metal desk. They could see smoke rising from his cigarette.

"The present work involves sound signals," Ken was explaining. "Dolphins have very acute hearing, much better than ours. We're converting hand signals to sound signals. Aphrodite understands sentences in hand signals, and she's learning the corresponding sounds. We're also computing those sound signals into visual signals that flash onto an underwater screen in a code of lights. The idea is to devise a way for dolphins not only to receive messages by computer, but to send them, as well."

"So it has nothing to do with teaching them English."

"No. I've devoted years of study to decoding dolphins' various sounds, many of which are out of range of human hearing. It's not unusual for dolphins to imitate human words, but attempting to teach them English is impractical, if not impossible. Their voice apparatus is nothing like ours. The only intelligent approach is to invent an entirely new language, on computers, which we and they learn together. This is what Brian and I are doing."

When Ken knocked on the window glass, Brian looked up from his work, set down his pencil and rose to join them, his tanned head shining in the afternoon sun and his tinted glasses catching light reflections from the pool. Adrienne greeted him warmly, but as they talked, she could not keep her eyes from wandering to the water, where Aphrodite and Ulysses were cavorting.

How mysterious all this was—this cooperation between two species so different from each other! It made her keenly aware of how much of life was still unknown, how much was left to learn.

She asked, "Is complex communication really possible? Are dolphins as intelligent as some people claim?"

"More," Ken answered. "Often they learn faster than we do. Sometimes I wonder how they tolerate our limitations."

Brian grinned. "Ken gets flack constantly from scientists over statements like the one he just made. So he's trying to set up an experimental program at the university to prove that humans under the same conditions and disadvantages and environmental changes can't learn as fast as cetaceans. Especially the orca."

"A hopeless experiment," Ken said with a sigh. "The conditions are impossible to duplicate. What I'd really like to prove with it is that some scientists are as guilty of preclusions about human intelligence as they accuse me of being about cetacean intelligence."

Brian wiped perspiration from his forehead. "Did you see our baby, Adrienne? We're excited about it! Three women have volunteered to let their kids swim with the dolphin for a couple of hours a day, to see what the babies learn from each other. We've never had a chance to work with such a young dolphin before."

Adrienne felt, once again, a sharp stab of envy. No wonder these men were so absorbed in their work; there was no end to its fascination. "I've just met one of your volunteer kids," she said, smiling. "Kevin Summers."

"Kev and the baby tursiops just met," Ken said. "Or at least they saw each other. Jillie swam in close. She was so curious about Kevin she slowed almost to a stop to look him over."

The more Adrienne listened to Ken, the more she understood him. Ken Burke was essentially a loner, isolated from humans, totally immersed in another world. What he had offered to share with her had nothing to do with him personally. Except, she recalled with the heat of the memory scorching her, those two magical kisses. He had been different then, that night of the kisses, with runaway human passions, passions she had relived a thousand times.

Today, except for his moments of anxiety over her unexplained behavior, except for the concern in his eyes at the poolside, he was treating her like a visiting diplomat. Polite and businesslike, he kept a little distance from her, as though getting too close were against some rule. Yet he had wanted to share the excitement of the dolphin's birth with her. What she ought to do, Adrienne told herself with fierce determination, was to forget about those soft and fiery kisses. Ken obviously had.

6

LATE THAT EVENING Ken took two beers from the refrigerator in his tiny apartment and handed one to his colleague. He slouched onto the sofa and sipped slowly.

Brian kicked off his rubber thongs and stretched out on the floor. "What's the story with Adrienne and the dolphins, Ken?"

"Well, as you know, some of the dolphins take an unusual interest in her. It's one of the strangest things I've ever seen—Adrienne's rapport with Aphrodite. Even Ulysses perked up and took an interest in everything Adrienne was doing when..." He stopped short.

Brian's eyebrows raised. "Yeah? When what?"

"Never mind."

"You let her get in their pool, you old dog!"

"It's not what you think. She acted so disappointed when I refused that I weakened. Anyhow, it was more or less an experiment. After the way Aphrodite took to Adrienne that first day, I wanted to see her reaction when someone besides me got into the pool."

"Just scientific, huh? Sure!"

Ken ran his fingers through his hair. "You should have seen them in the water, Brian. Like two long-lost friends. There was something between them that I couldn't understand...something almost mystical. Adrienne has to be conveying subconscious messages to both Aphrodite and Ulysses, but I've talked with her enough to know that she has no idea what those messages are."

The older man sipped absently at his beer. "It's as plain as feathers on a foul that you're attracted to her."

"Well, she's a beautiful woman." Ken leaned back against the sofa cushions and closed his eyes. Adrienne was there when he closed his eyes; since the night he had kissed her and felt the response of her body to his, she was always there when he closed his eyes. His hand slid over his arm where her nails had left their marks. What had been going on in Adrienne's mind, he wondered, when she saw the baby in the dolphin pool? Something had terrified her, and he had wanted to hold her, comfort her.

But he hadn't. Whether it was because he was afraid of her or of himself, he wasn't sure. What he did know was that the memory of their kiss flew down on him a hundred times a day at the least-expected moments. This moment....

Ken knew the signs of danger. Unchecked, that fire smoldering just below the surface when the two of them were close could burn wildly out of control.

Brian's loud voice startled him. "When you came into the lounge last night Adrienne looked at you as if she were seeing her first sunrise. Just the same way she looks at the dolphins."

Ken frowned at this.

"You didn't notice?"

The dark-blue eyes wandered away, stared at the wall, then looked back helplessly at Brian. "She's a concert pianist."

"What does that have to do with anything?"

Ken gave a disheartened shrug. "It ought to be obvious."

"I'll tell you what's obvious—she might be just what you're looking for. Adrienne Canaday is a very rich lady!"

"I doubt it. If she were rich she wouldn't be working in a lounge."

Brian wiped a line of beer foam from his mustache. "Yeah? I was partying with her cousin last night. You remember Cousin Carmen? She told me your friend is heiress to a very impressive fortune."

Ken sighed heavily. "Maybe your memory is hazy. You were sloshed last night."

"So was Carmen. That's why she was talking so much. I'm telling you, Ken, Adrienne is rich!"

"Well, maybe it figures. She certainly looks the part. But what difference does it make?"

Brian waved an arm impatiently. "Don't you see what this could mean, man? It's the miracle we've been praying for! If you married an heiress, our troubles would be over!"

Ken Burke's eyes turned ice-cold as they stared at his closest friend. "Brian, are you crazy?"

"I'm dead serious! You like her! She's beautiful. Think about what it would mean to us!"

Ken glared. "What I'm thinking about is your burst of insanity. I hope it's temporary."

"Come on, Ken! You said yourself we needed a miracle. You've got that look on your face I hate—like you just ate something putrid. Is it so unthinkable you might fall in love with Adrienne?"

Ken didn't answer for a long time while he gazed at the floor without any expression at all. Finally he took a huge swallow from his can of beer and said huskily, "No, it's not unthinkable I could fall in love with her! It is unthinkable that I'd ever marry her."

Brian's face reddened through his deep tan, as if he were on the verge of exploding. "Why? Just because she has money?"

"Because I don't have money. Adrienne Canaday is obviously used to a style of living I could never give her. I couldn't live with that! I've been through it once before, Brian. My ex-wife constantly prodded me to get into another line of work. It was either provide for my family 'properly' or give up what I'd wanted all my life. She was from a wealthy family, too, used to all the things I could never give her."

Brian guzzled his beer, his head back, his Adam's apple moving as he swallowed. He set down the empty can. "So I suppose you'll end up with a girl like Melanie Stevens, who doesn't own a dress and whose highest goal in life is to ride on a killer whale at Sea World."

Ken shrugged. "At least Melanie might adjust to my life-style. Adrienne never could."

"Adrienne wouldn't have to. She can have whatever she wants, and I have the feeling she wants you."

"She's too smart for that. Her interest is strictly in dolphins."

"You wouldn't consider marrying her? Even if it meant being able to keep the lab?"

"Hell, no!" Anger flashed in Ken's eyes. "What kind of guy do you think I am, Brian?" He rose abruptly and opened the side door that led into the indoor pool. His presence was greeted with little beeping sounds from the inhabitants of the pool. The water was dark, but he could see their shadows as they swam, the attentive mother at her baby's side. The smell of the pool, the smell of the night closed around him, and he felt a poignant sadness. Thoughts of Adrienne tore at him with claws of rippling pain, launching undefined, distorted barbs of loneliness, or something like loneliness.

He thought he knew Brian after working with him for eight years. He had supposed Brian knew him. But this? The confrontation had left Ken trembling with anger.

Involuntarily his mind kept calling back the candle-lit picture of Adrienne in shimmering black, her delicately beautiful face with its small, expressive mouth and eyes as pale as a winter sky. Slim, manicured fingers on the keyboard. He thought about the scars on her left hand, scars she didn't want to talk about—testimonies to pain long past.

The mother dolphin jumped, flipping her flukes like a giant fan, splashing him, bringing him back to stark reality—a very different reality from Adrienne's. He could hear Brian shuffling about the apartment, opening and closing the refrigerator door. As if his anger with Brian weren't enough, there was all the rest to cope with: the added weight of knowing Adrienne was as wealthy as she was beautiful and talented and charming—one of those privileged few who was born with everything.

Ken turned to go back inside. Brian must be getting senile, he decided. It was frightening what desperation could do to a man's mental health. Of course, exploitation is easy when it's someone else's life you're manipulating. But even Brian ought to understand that the death of pride was a living death.

ALTHOUGH ADRIENNE watched for him each night, Ken did not return to the Sea Cliff. And each night her disappointment deepened. Days fell slowly into a second week. To her it seemed almost a dream, thinking back, that he had ever held her, ever kissed her at all. Yet his kisses were engraved in her memory. The taste of him, the feel of him never left her. Sometimes she saw his face in those misty moments between waking and sleeping, and she awoke sinking in the emptiness of knowing he wasn't there.

Brian appeared at the Sea Cliff lounge on a Friday night with Melanie Stevens. They chose a table near the piano, and after Adrienne had finished the set, Brian waved her over.

"Join us for a few minutes, Adrienne. Have a drink with us. Do you know Melanie?"

"Yes, we've met." Smiling, she sat down and ordered a cup of tea from the waitress.

Brian asked, "Have you heard from Ken this week?"

"No."

"I guess nobody has. He's home on his boat, sulking."

"He hasn't been at work?"

Brian gulped his drink, then set down the glass with a hard click on the tabletop. "You didn't hear what happened?"

A small fear fluttered through her as she shook her head.

Melanie's one long, auburn braid fell forward when she leaned across the table. "Ken was installing some electronic equipment on a high platform, when the platform gave way. He broke his arm in the fall."

Adrienne drew a quick breath in a reflex of shock. Soft folds of gray chiffon flowed in the light as she raised her hand to her throat. She looked at Brian.

"He's lucky one arm is all he broke," Brian said. "Though he sure did a thorough job on it. All three bones fractured. And the other arm is badly sprained. He landed on concrete, trying to protect the delicate equipment he was holding." Grinning, he looked at Melanie, then back to Adrienne. "You should see him with one arm and shoulder in a cast and the other arm in bandages. He looks like King Tut."

"That's terrible!"

"Believe it's terrible. We're at a crucial point in our work, and this has brought us to a standstill."

The waitress brought Adrienne a little black teapot.

Brian continued, "I offered to pick him up and drive him to the lab today, but he said no. He isn't finished with his royal sulk yet."

"Don't be so hard on him," Melanie said, sipping a pink drink through a straw. "How would you feel if you had to try to dress and feed yourself with only half a hand?"

"You're right. He's not a happy man. Can't work with Aphrodite because he has no arms for the signals, and she's so temperamental she won't work consistently for me. The two of them started out together on this project, and Aphrodite thinks he's deserted her. Hell, Ken can't even work the computers until his arm gets better." He leaned back and gulped his drink as though the world were at an end.

Adrienne gazed into her teacup. Perhaps Ken would have come in to see her if he hadn't been hurt; maybe he wasn't avoiding her, after all. Did she only imagine

Brian's exaggerated eagerness to let her know Ken was having a rough time? Cautiously she asked, "Is he alone on his boat?"

"Sure. If you're asking how he's feeling or how he's managing by himself, I wouldn't know." He drained his glass, gazing at her over the rim. "Things are sure falling apart at the lab with Ken gone. We're way behind schedule. I trust he'll come back soon, but it'll be weeks before he gets that cast off. What he needs is someone to dictate notes to, record things for him. Melanie could, if she weren't so overloaded with work already."

Adrienne could see through Brian Palmer; he was clearly setting her up. She had been puzzled at first, but now the reason seemed clear. He hoped she would volunteer to help. Maybe she should, but only if Ken wanted her help.

Even before she sat down at the piano again, people were requesting songs. For the rest of that evening she found it hard to concentrate on the music, because her thoughts kept drifting back to Ken.

IN THE MORNING she drove to Shelter Island. It was a cloudy day that promised rain. By the time she reached the marina it was drizzling. Following Brian's directions, Adrienne walked out onto the center pier, pulling her windbreaker tighter around her as wind whipped at her white cotton skirt, chilling her legs. Masts rose up around her like swaying trees. Strong was the scent of sea and boats and ropes. Water lapped against the pilings of the pier and the boat hulls. Vessels pulled restlessly at their moorings as if they were eager for the open sea and tired of the confinement of the harbor.

Ken's boat was easy enough to find. Moored midway down the pier, it was a white cruiser with blue trim and the name *Firefly* printed in blue letters across the transom. The boat was bigger than she had expected, and older, though it looked well cared for. A light shone through red-curtained portholes.

The drizzle had turned to rain, but even in the downpour, Adrienne paused on the catwalk, wishing she had phoned first to let him know she was coming. Maybe he didn't want her to come. He'd have said no, and that would have been the end of it, and she could have spared her pride.

The rain chilled her, penetrating her jacket, soaking her hair. Yet for more than a minute she stood looking at the boat, thinking murky thoughts and absently rubbing the scars of her left hand, unable to understand these macabre sensations that seemed inextricably linked to boats.

It was a sort of fear. Not the kind that brought ragged shivers to the skin, but a deep, hard-frozen inner fear that never quite thawed, no matter how many times she sailed. So many of her mother's friends had yachts, and, with great effort, Adrienne had learned to suppress the nagging pangs. She would climb aboard on trembling legs, and usually, once there and absorbed in activities, she could keep the anxiety at bay.

The years had helped contain this bloodless, meaningless fear of boats. Yet strangely, today in the rain, facing Ken's softly rocking cruiser, she felt very close to losing that control. Terror—old and rancid terror— came whirling back on flaps of crippled time.

Adrienne gripped her handbag tightly and raised her eyes to the weeping skies, letting the rain splash on her face while she forced back the unwelcome emotions. The only danger at hand was making a fool of herself. The incident with Kevin in the pool had been bad enough. She had to mobilize the power of her inner strength. It had always worked before.

Wet and chilled, she stepped from the catwalk onto the deck, reaching for the railing. A gust of wind nearly blew her off balance as her sandals skidded on the deck. "Permission to come aboard?"

Ken appeared at the hatch entrance, barefoot, wearing cutoff jeans and no shirt. His right arm, encased in plaster from wrist to shoulder, rested in a sling; his left was bandaged from the elbow down, leaving only half his hand free. A shaggy beard and an unfamiliar, lifeless expression in his eyes made him seem a stranger— and one who didn't seem particularly pleased to see her.

She stepped down the three steps into the cabin. "Ken, you look terrible!"

He moved back, easing himself onto a cushioned bunk. "I meant to spare you the sight."

"Why? We're friends, aren't we? I hope you don't think I'm too lightweight to qualify as a friend of yours."

When he didn't answer at once, she looked about the cabin, at its teak floors and dark-paneled ceiling. A center table divided a small galley on one side from the lounge area on the other, where they stood now. High shelves held an impressive collection of books behind carved leather straps. Stacks of papers and magazines and assorted clothes created general clutter, similar to the state of the apartment at the lab.

Ken finally answered with a question. "Are you saying this visit has to do with friendship?"

She rolled her eyes upward, hands on her hips. "Well, what else would it have to do with? Trying to cheer up grouchy shut-ins isn't a hobby of mine. Obviously you haven't thought of me as a friend."

"I guess I haven't, exactly."

"Is there some reason why you can't start now?"

His voice softened. "No reason I can think of."

"Good." Her eyes traveled over his cast. "Too bad you aren't able to shake on it." Without an invitation to do so, Adrienne unzipped her wet windbreaker and peeled the limp sleeves from her arms.

"There's a towel for your hair in the galley," he offered. "Top drawer on the left."

She found it, hung her dripping jacket on a hook and sat down across from him, her head hanging as she patted her hair with the towel. "Do you feel as awful as you look?"

She heard an unintelligible curse. "This is really embarrassing, Adrienne. I've been in ridiculous predicaments before, but nothing to rival this. Until my hand gets better I can't even drive."

"You're in pain, aren't you? I can tell."

"It comes and goes." He cleared his throat. "I'm surprised to see you."

"I know."

"You've been one surprise after another, Adrienne, ever since I met you."

A long pause. She knew he was watching her dry her hair and probably wondering why she didn't dress more sensibly to go out in the rain.

"You can grab a shirt from that pile of clean laundry if you want. Your blouse is pretty wet."

From behind the towel, Adrienne thought she detected a note of nervousness in his voice. "I will, if you don't mind. I seem to have trouble staying dry around you."

"Are you cold?"

"I can survive anything. Always have." She threw the towel aside and stood up to take off her blouse. Then, in her half-dry lavender lace bra, she searched through his pile of clothes and pulled out a tattered gray sweat shirt.

Ken grinned cautiously. "Now I know how harmless and pathetic I must look. You didn't even hesitate to undress in front of me."

"You sure do look harmless. You look different, too, with the beard."

"Shaving is damn near impossible, along with everything else."

She was rubbing her arms, warming them through the soft cotton flannel of his sweat shirt. "I could help you."

He scowled. "Help me shave?"

She flushed. Of course she hadn't meant shave, but she answered bravely, "Why not? I once had a course in first aid. I know exactly what to do if I accidentally slit your throat."

"Never mind. I need the beard. The derelict look matches my mood."

"Brian was right. He said you were sulking."

"I've got plenty to sulk about. Are you serious about the offer to help?"

"Sure. I'm no good at shorthand, but my typing isn't too bad...."

He shook his head. "I don't need a secretary, I need a nurse. I thought your offer was a little more personal."

Adrienne had to let this remark sink in while she studied the plaster and the bandages. With one arm totally immobile and the other stiffly bandaged from elbow to fingers, he did look as helpless as he complained of being. She struggled to keep her voice even. "My offer was sincere." It was sincere, but what did he mean by "personal"?

"I've got problems you wouldn't believe," Ken moaned. "I can't take a shower with this cast. Just for starters."

Her knees went weak. He was teasing her again. He had to be. Okay, she'd play. "I could take a shower for you, if..." She stopped. He wasn't teasing—not with that helpless look on his face. She swallowed. "Can you bathe?"

"Yeah. I run five inches of water in the shower stall and sit in it. But please don't try to picture that. Could you find my dilemma pitiful enough to offer to wash my back for me?"

Of course she was picturing him sitting naked in the shower stall. That was why her voice trembled when she answered, "Sure...I could...wash your back."

"I feel like an invalid," he said sourly.

"You are a temporary invalid of sorts, so I'll throw in a back rub. As tense as you look right now, you could use one."

Their eyes met. "You'd really do all that for me?"

"Sure, since we're friends. Where are the washcloths?"

He looked suddenly doubtful, embarrassed. "Adrienne, you really don't have to do this. I was half kidding."

"No, you weren't. Don't worry so much. This I can handle."

Moments later she was standing before him with a soapy cloth and a pan of water. "Okay, turn around. We must be careful not to get the cast wet."

He obeyed in submissive silence. "Umm. That feels good."

"How could it? It's cold water. Don't you have any hot?"

"No. Who needs hot water?"

"Right," she said, cringing. "Who does?" Slowly, as slowly as possible, she washed his neck and his back, savoring the feel of his skin, even through the wet cloth, while he mumbled little praises of appreciation. She rinsed, then dried his back, rubbing briskly with a towel, letting her fingertips linger on the hard muscles of his shoulders. "You are tense. Can't you at least try to relax?"

"Not when you're..." He changed his mind about whatever it was he'd intended to say and muttered instead, "I'm trying."

"Maybe if you lie down..."

"This damned cast keeps me from lying on my stomach."

Sympathy softened her voice. "That's part of the problem, Ken. You can't get comfortable. Can't we find a way to get you comfortable?"

"Hmm, I don't know. Can we?"

Adrienne was thrown off balance when he used that certain tone—that raspy mumble that sounded like a prelude to sex. Her stomach tightened and shuddered intermittently. She raised on wobbly knees to reach his neck and shoulders and began to massage the tight muscles. Ken had to sit straight while she did this, pushing back against her hands. He couldn't even lean over to use his arms for support.

"You're still not comfortable. You couldn't be. There must be some way you can lie down. What about on your side?"

"I can try."

He shifted around with a great deal of grunting, until he was lying on his good shoulder on the narrow bunk, facing away from her.

Adrienne tucked a pillow under his head. Then she slid to the floor, to her knees, and leaned around his broad shoulders. "Is that better?"

"Yeah. But I'll never get up."

"Oh, well, one obstacle at a time." Her tingling fingers found their way up and down the curves and ridges of his back, up along his neck and across his shoulders.

He moaned, subdued. "That feels incredibly good. My neck is still stiff from the fall."

Adrienne was touched by his surrender to his own needs. Several days alone with the frustration and discomfort had taken their toll. His armor had rusted a little—at least enough for him to admit he needed someone, if only for a little while...if only for this.

Her fingers kneaded the muscles of his back. He mumbled about how strong her hands were, and she reminded him that she was a pianist.

Ken drew up one knee, wiggling to get more comfortable. On her knees, Adrienne explored every inch of his back as she massaged his skin skillfully, feeling him begin to relax. She was anything but relaxed. His shorts were so tight over his hips it was hard to keep her eyes off them. His well-muscled legs were a temptation; she would love to touch his legs, to massage him all over. And Ken wouldn't mind. But if she did and he got excited...well, what?

Well, nothing. The heavy cast weighted him down, rendered him about sixty percent helpless, not counting his other bandaged arm. What lousy luck! Here she was on a boat, with the sexiest man she had ever met lying before her nearly naked, and he could barely move!

She decided to try conversation. "Will you go back to work soon?"

"I'm worthless at the lab. I think I'll just sit and grow moss."

"Moss grows profusely on self-pity."

"I'll be a living moss ball, then."

"Brian says if you had help at the lab..."

"Don't pay any attention to Brian. He talks too much."

"You don't need help?"

"No, I don't need anything." He yawned, then moaned with pleasure at the pressure of her touch. "Yes, I do. I need this back rub. You're an angel."

"I think I'm putting you to sleep."

He was apologetic. "I may fall asleep. I haven't been this comfortable in days...haven't slept well at all..."

"Go to sleep, then, Ken."

"Don't want to. I'll miss my back rub."

Unexpectedly he turned over, grunting, onto his back, and looked at her with sadness in his eyes—a strange sadness laced with longing. She drew closer, brushing his thick hair back from his forehead, touching his beard with the back of her fingers. His eyes told her what his hands could not. His one half-working arm urged her toward his lips, to a kiss so tender Adrienne could feel the waves of it tremble through the depths of her being. It was more than just a kiss, more than passion, more than gratitude, more than friendship. More than all of them combined. And it left her confused and breathless.

Seconds tumbled over seconds as he gazed into her eyes, touching the ends of her hair with bandaged fingers. The boat rocked in the gentle sway of the tides. Music of rain played steadily on the roof. Adrienne knew she wanted this man in a different way, an aching way, and his eyes were all the testimony she needed that he wanted her, too.

He sighed shakily and his eyes closed. When she moved, his eyes opened, then closed again.

"Ken? What's wrong? You don't feel very well, do you?"

"Not too well. Maybe I'm just tired."

"Then rest. Do you want anything before I go?"

His eyes half opened once more. "That's a dangerous question."

"Not too dangerous, from the looks of you."

"That's because the back rub felt so good I relaxed past the point of no return."

Smiling, she leaned down to kiss his forehead.

For some time—uncounted time—Adrienne sat on the bench across from Ken, listening to the rain on the roof and the small moans and creaks that made the boat seem alive. The plaster cast looked very white against his tanned skin, white and heavy, and it moved with the rhythm of his breathing. His hair curled over his fore-head. His bare legs twitched slightly from time to time. He had drifted easily into swift, deep sleep. Healing sleep.

Snuggled in the warmth of his sweat shirt, she watched, and waited for the rain to stop. Was he really the best-looking man she had ever known, or was it only the way she saw him? It amounted to the same thing either way: helpless attraction. The longer she stayed near him, the harder it was going to be to leave. Yet something inside her knew she would have to leave sometime. And not because of her. Because of him.

7

THE SKIES WERE DARK ALL WEEK, and rain continued to fall intermittently from low storm clouds. Streets were pale rivers; waxy palm leaves bent in wind. On the freeway, driving home from La Jolla after midnight, Adrienne's mood was as turbulent as the dancing swirls in the yellow cone of light in front of her. Lately the nights had surrounded her with soggy blackness.

The days were gray and drizzly, and grayer still because of Ken's silence.

Nine days passed before he phoned her early one evening at the Sea Cliff. His voice sounded even deeper on the phone than in person, and he didn't bother with the expected polite trivia. "I'm going insane, Adrienne. I lied when I said I didn't need you."

She felt a rush of blood to her head, and some of the feeling went out of the hand that was holding the telephone. She struggled for control of her voice. "Are you growing moss on your back?"

"Probably. I haven't seen my back lately. But this is more life threatening. Brian and I are having a hell of a time because I can't work with one arm. Were you...?" His voice became very soft, embarrassed. He cleared his throat.

She leaped in to help him, tingling with excitement before it was logical to get excited. "Do you need help with the dolphins?"

His voice strengthened. "If you have any extra time, I'd sure like to see if Aphrodite would be willing to work with you. Brian is having problems with her. I realize it's a tremendous favor to ask of anyone..."

"Who is doing whom the favor?"

"Then you'll do it? Can you come tomorrow?"

She was trembling. "Of course tomorrow. I'm free until six-thirty, when I have to be here at the lounge. Ken?"

"Yeah?"

"What about Ulysses? Will I be working with him, too?"

"Probably not. He's too independent. I'd have given the old boy his freedom long ago if he weren't so far from his home. He was captured off the coast of Florida. I told you about his attitude to humans. He carries a longtime grudge."

"Oh, I'm looking forward to tomorrow!"

"So am I," Ken said. "I've missed you."

It was a strange twist of fate, Adrienne thought, that she would have this chance. And yet, in a way, it was not strange, for she had felt some entwined destiny with dolphins from the first moment she saw them, felt a terrible longing to know them. Perhaps it was possible now, because of Ken's accident. He might have chosen Melanie or someone else to help him, but he hadn't. He had opened the door of his world to her, a world unlike any she had ever seen or imagined—a world of interspecies communication based on mutual respect, and love.

Her mother's house in Boston was empty now, save
for the housekeeper. All the plans she and Richard
made by his fireplace last winter were lost and,
strangely, almost forgotten. The world had turned on
its axis; dark had changed to light. Love had seeped
back so quickly through the cracks of mourning; it
shimmered like the sun of her new world and almost
scared her with its brilliance.

BY HER SIXTH DAY at the laboratory for cetacean studies, Adrienne had learned all the hand signals. Brian
had demonstrated each of them for her, and she and
Ken had named them, so he could tell her what he
wanted her to do. The dolphin, anxious to work again,
had cooperated with Adrienne from the first moment,
and all was going well. They were using the underwater screens, coded in lights, and the dolphin was beginning to show more interest in the screen, catching on to
the idea that the lights, too, were symbols of communication with human beings.

On this day Aphrodite had been lying on her side
during the break, watching the humans as if she
understood everything they said.

"We're projecting significant successes within five
years," Ken was saying to Adrienne. "Dolphins see so
much better underwater than above water that once
they begin to decode the computer, it will be much easier for them than our crude hand signals are. We'll use
just the sound and sight then, like a written and an au-
ditory language."

"What we expect," Brian said, "is that once the con-
cept of sending messages back to us is picked up by

Aphrodite, the others will learn from her. They have a complex language of their own."

"Can you be so certain they will want to do it?"

"No, but they give every indication of wanting to communicate with us."

"It's almost too much to comprehend! Are other labs doing this, too?"

"Sure, a few around the world, using various approaches. We worry about military exploitation."

Ken rose from the bench at the side of the pool. He was clean shaven again. The heavy bandages on his left arm had diminished to a small bandage around his sprained wrist, although abrasions on his upper arm were still visible. By now the cast was no longer glistening white, and it was defaced with signatures and cartoons.

He said, "Adrienne, let's try something. Signal to Aphrodite that you would be happy if you had the new rubber ring. Don't ask her to bring it to you. Just convey that you'd be happy if you could have it."

"She won't understand that," Brian insisted. "You're getting into expressions of emotion. We haven't figured out—"

"Let's try it, anyway, using the pleasure signal you use when you tell Aphrodite she has done a good job and pleased you. Go ahead, Adrienne."

Aware of the men's eyes on her as she stood in white shorts and a bikini top, Adrienne took her place on the short platform that extended over the water. By now the California sun had bronzed her skin and lightened her blond hair.

Aphrodite questioned the change in signals, but only for a moment or two. Then she swam to the opposite side of the pool, chose the blue rubber ring from the several objects in the pool, slipped it over her beaklike snout and brought it to Adrienne, who rewarded her with pats, praises and a mackerel and asked her to hang it on a hook on the opposite side of the enclosure.

At the computer, Brian called, "That was fantastic! I'm going to repeat this command using only sound and screen patterns. No hands this time. Let's just see what she does."

Although she swam near the screen several times, Aphrodite didn't seem to be picking up the message. She studied the screen and looked at Adrienne, then lay on the surface quite still, waiting for something more. Brian kept repeating the signals. Ulysses was looking on passively, as always. Sometimes he showed some interest in the activities; other times he would rush by with an attitude of disdain.

Now, unexpectedly, the large male dolphin made a swift, underwater circle around the pool, rose up to the hook and looped the rubber ring around his snout. With impatient up-and-down motions, he swam to Adrienne, lifted his enormous silver head out of the water and flung the ring into the air in her direction.

With startled reflex Adrienne was able to reach out in time to catch the ring. She held it in front of her, stunned, as she watched Ulysses plunge back into the deep end, shunning the idea of a reward. Moments later he seemed to change his mind, for he returned and allowed her to pat his head and sing him praises. But he refused the fish she offered.

Brian was hopping around, making apelike chirps. Ken was uncharacteristically silent as he observed Ulysses carefully, but Adrienne could see a fire of wild excitement shining in his dark-blue eyes. Ulysses, quickly bored with the attention and the hoopla, swam to the deep end of the pool, ignoring the humans with his usual air of indifference. Adrienne jumped down from the platform, smiling, still carrying the blue ring.

"You did it!" Ken grinned. "You broke the barrier with Ulysses! You're the only one who could have done it!"

Brian grabbed the ring and waved it in the air, dancing in circles. "That old barnacle back knows exactly what's going on! You were right about him all along, Ken!"

"This doesn't mean he's going to start cooperating with us. But it does mean his desire to please Adrienne was strong enough to break down his defense!" He turned to Brian. "Ulysses became very impatient with Aphrodite when she didn't get the signals. Did you notice? This supports what I've suspected all along—the two of them have been doing our routines at night, when no one is around."

"This calls for a celebration!" Brian said with a whoop. He placed the ring around Adrienne's neck. "Here, love! A present from Ulysses! He sure was determined you should have it."

Still tingling with the thrill of the incredible phenomenon that had just occurred, Adrienne grabbed her shirt from the bench, and the three of them walked over the winding sidewalk to Ken's small living quarters in the main building. This Saturday afternoon there was no one else around. Shadows of the trees slanted over green lawns. A few clouds had gathered high in the sky, and the air was beginning to cool.

Brian took three beers from Ken's refrigerator and passed them around. With her white shirt wrapped around her, Adrienne sat on the couch, stroking the thick rubber ring Brian had placed around her neck. "I've never been so thrilled over a gift in my life!"

"The ring of Ulysses," Ken mused, settling himself into a chair. "According to Greek mythology, Ulysses himself always wore a ring with the figure of a dolphin on it. A tribute to dolphins who saved his son from drowning."

"I remember!" Adrienne said with a smile, her pale eyes shining. "My mother often told me that story of Ulysses' ring. She was particularly fascinated by it."

Ken set his beer can on the floor beside his chair. "Greek mythology started my interest in dolphins when I was a kid. I was intrigued with the stories of friendship between dolphins and humans. I still am. I've never discovered the reason for it."

"Do you think the dolphins know the reason for it?" she asked.

He looked at her with new understanding, an expression that acknowledged that only a person who knew dolphins could ask such a question. "They might know. They've been on this old spinning planet a lot longer than we have, and I'm sure they understand it better."

THE FOLLOWING DAY, a bright warm Sunday, Ulysses feigned amnesia, and would take no part in the activities. But his shining eyes were on the humans all the time. Often during that short afternoon session with Aphrodite, private exchanges of pings and beeps took place between the two dolphins.

It was midafternoon when a siren sounded down-shore, toward La Jolla. The shrill disaster warning swelled long and loud in the still, sun-sweet air. Absorbed in their work Ken and Brian gave the sirens little thought, assuming they were only tests, until the telephone began ringing. Brian left his post at the computer and sprinted to the office to answer.

Adrienne and Ken met him on the path as he rushed back, out of breath. "We've got a tidal-wave warning! Started from an earthquake in Japan, moving across the Pacific. The Hawaiian Islands were hit fifteen minutes ago and are reporting major damage, expecting more. The wave is expected to reach California in four or five hours."

Ken's eyes conveyed the concern his voice did not. "The cliff should protect the lab from any damage. It would have to be a hell of a wave to reach this high."

"No, we shouldn't have a problem here," Brian agreed. "But you'd better get your butt down to the marina."

Ken began to swear under his breath. "Of all the times for this to happen. With me half helpless."

"I'll go with you. We'll manage."

Scowling, Ken shifted the sling. "You have to stay, Brian. Somebody has to be here."

"You can't get your boat out of its mooring with one hand! You can barely drive a car."

"I'll drive you to the marina," Adrienne offered, "And I've steered boats before. But I don't understand why you want to move it, or where."

"To the open ocean," Ken answered. "If a tidal wave hits, boats in the harbor could be smashed to splinters. The safest place is on top of the wave, on the high sea."

"It sounds dangerous."

"Only the beach areas are dangerous. It's too soon to panic, though. This could be a false alarm."

"It was no false alarm in Hawaii," Brian reminded him. "And if it hits here, you could lose your boat."

A sudden cool breeze flapped at the tails of Adrienne's open shirt. She pulled it around her and buttoned it. "I'll help. You can tell me what needs to be done, and I'll do it."

Ken grinned. "Offer accepted, Adrienne. There's nobody with whom I'd rather ride out a tidal wave."

This pleased her more than anything he'd ever said to her. "I'll just get my jeans and jacket from the bathhouse and call Carmen to let her know where I am so she won't worry."

There was tension in the air at the marina, and much more activity than usual for a Sunday afternoon. Walking the length of the pier, Adrienne and Ken could hear speculations all around them about the impending danger. They had no sooner boarded Ken's thirty-four-foot cruiser than a bearded man in a white captain's cap called out from the deck of a tall-masted sloop on the portside. "Hey, Burke, what the devil happened to you?"

Ken shrugged and grinned at his neighbors, a handsome middle-aged couple. "Had a little accident at work."

The woman, in shorts and sweat shirt, moved to the railing. "Well, even with a broken arm, you're the experienced sailor, Ken! Advise us what to do. We're loosening the starboard lines and tightening the port lines."

Ken rubbed his chin with his free hand. "Too much starboard line could allow her to swing under the catwalk. When the water rises again after the drop, she could be crushed underneath. On the other hand, if the lines are too tight, they could snap if the water drops too much. It's hard to predict exactly what the sea will do, but I'd fasten on all the fenders you've got and put on a spring line. But it'll still be a gamble if you plan to sit it out here."

The man pushed his cap back. "I talked to a Coast Guard officer. He said they'll make us evacuate if the news keeps getting worse. Can they do that?"

"We'd be crazy not to evacuate if it comes to that, Cooper."

"What are you going to do?"

"Check my fuel and make sure everything's battened down in case we have to haul ass out of here."

"Leave the harbor? That's what you'd advise?"

"It's what every seaworthy boat will be doing."

"That's what we'd better do then, Harve," the woman interjected, sounding worried.

"Yeah..." He gazed at the younger couple on the *Firefly*'s polished deck. "How are you going to manage with one arm, Burke? Do you need some help?"

"Yeah, I could use a hand with the lines in a little while."

"You got it. Give a holler."

Ken thanked his neighbors and hurriedly introduced Adrienne to them while he was fumbling at the front pocket of his tight jeans and wincing. They were standing in front of the locked cabin door. His wincing deteriorated to soft swearing.

She asked, "What's the matter?"

"My wrist is still sore as hell. I can't get the keys out of my pocket. I need help."

A blush of heat appeared on Adrienne's cheeks. "You expect me to get my hand in the pocket of those tight jeans? Are you sure you can't get your keys out yourself?"

"Did you ever try to get your hand into a tight pocket with a sprained wrist?"

She groaned in mock defeat.

He said, "Just be careful. I'm ticklish there."

The Coopers were still talking and looking their way. Adrienne tried to be casual, glancing past Ken to the sloop next door as she burrowed two trembling fingers into his pocket. She couldn't reach the keys.

Muttering little phrases that barely resembled English, she withdrew her hand and tried again, this time wriggling in four fingers. She was praying he wouldn't notice the trembling. "Ken, must you squirm? Do you know how awful this looks?"

"It doesn't feel too bad."

She flushed and wouldn't look up at him. "How did you ever get these keys in here in the first place?"

"I put them in the pocket before I put my pants on. I can get them out the same way, but it may look even a lot worse than what we're doing now."

"Nevertheless there may not be any other choice. And if you ask me, dropping your pants couldn't look much worse from the Coopers' boat than this!"

"Yes, it could. I don't wear underpants."

This was too much! The cotton material lining his pocket suddenly felt incredibly thin to the touch. "You don't...?" Her voice jammed with such heavy hoarseness that she had to start again—with self-discipline and with her hand still inside his pocket and the keys still farther down. "You don't wear underwear?"

"Only for formal occasions."

"Why not?"

"Because my clothes get wet all the time. The fewer clothes I have on the better."

She swallowed and struggled to control her voice. "I wish you'd hold still! I can feel them." She finally got her fingers on his keys and tried to draw them out, but music from a radio on another neighboring boat suddenly filled the afternoon air.

Ken lunged backward unexpectedly, forcing Adrienne's arm and then the rest of her to follow. She had a death grip on the keys by now, but his pocket held almost as tight a hold on her hand. She nearly lost her balance as she stumbled forward.

"Ken, what the hell are you doing?" she swore through clenched teeth.

"The music," he answered in a casual tone that indicated he couldn't understand how she could ask anything so obvious. "Makes me feel like dancing." He had begun weaving sideways, keeping time with the music.

"I think I'll kill you!" she promised, stumbling awkwardly over her own feet. With a desperate tug, Adrienne was able to extract the keys and her hand from the warm and deep sanctuary of his thinly lined pocket.

Wanting to escape the eyes and laughter of the curious boaters as fast as possible, Adrienne turned to unlock the hatch door, fumbling awkwardly with the ring of keys. Ken watched her, saying nothing.

She muttered while she frantically tried one key, then another, "Next time you can get out your own damn keys, even if you have to drop your pants!"

"It has a red ring around it," he said flatly.

She stared at him. "What has?"

"The key."

Desperately she tried to suppress laughter, looking away from him as she sorted through the half-dozen keys to find the one with a narrow red band painted around the top. He made no further effort to be helpful.

Once inside the cabin, Adrienne exploded into fireworks of giggles. The key ring hit the wood tabletop with a metallic clank when she dropped it, then turned to face Ken, unstrung by his sorcery, powerless to control the consuming laughter. "How could you embarrass me like that?"

"Often I'm despicable. You don't look very mad."

"I'm trying to be mad, but the picture of me stumbling toward you with my hand stuck in your pocket as if I were...actually...trying..." Helpless giggling overtook her; she plopped onto the red-cushioned bench.

He frowned, the mischief still sparking in his blue eyes. "And if you were...actually...trying...well, I'd hope what you found in there wouldn't send you into gales of laughter!"

Her eyes met his to tell him silently, between the bursts of giggles, that if he had to tease her, to please find something else—anything else—to tease about. What defense did a woman have against this man's overpowering sexuality? When he was so damned aware of his sexuality! His suggestive remarks were like injections of adrenaline. He must know what he was doing to her with his deliberately tantalizing teasing, in spite of his smile of boyish innocence.

She would fight back, though, and try to keep the present in her control. "You admitted you're ticklish. I'm too ladylike to take advantage of your weakness, but I should have taken advantage when I had the perfect chance—when you were doing your klutzy tango on the deck. And here I was assuming this tidal-wave alert was serious business."

"Oh yeah, the tidal wave. Now I remember there is an ultralogical reason that you're here with me."

Adrienne glanced around the cluttered cabin. "Well, now that I'm here, what do we do? Stow things and prepare to cast off? I'll start by getting the dirty dishes washed and put away."

Ken turned on the radio. The announcer was reporting damages from two seismic-wave hits in the Hawaiian Islands. The Coast Guard had ordered all Southern California beach areas evacuated.

"Hell," he muttered, grabbing an armful of papers and dumping them into a cardboard box, which he kicked impatiently into a corner.

Adrienne stepped into the galley. "Don't worry. I work fast."

"I doubt there's any need to hurry. We should have a couple of safe hours left."

He went back out on deck, and from below Adrienne could hear voices out there, but it was difficult to tell what they were saying. She washed and stowed his few dishes without bothering to dry them, and then straightened the cabin. There wasn't much to do—the room was so small.

The panic that had taken such a hold on her the first time she came aboard Ken's boat hadn't surfaced at all today, on this sunny afternoon. So much had been occupying her mind—with Ken so near, and the sirens and the excitement of a dreaded tidal wave.

When she joined him on deck, he was on his knees, closing the raised engine hatch. "We have plenty of fuel. I keep her seaworthy, rev her up every few days."

She noticed he had pulled the overhead canopy back so that the bench at the stern was in the glare of bright west sun. Rippling harbor water sparkled around them. Masts swayed gently. Not a single boat was moving yet. Nothing in the peace of the late summer's day hinted at the wall of destruction moving slowly toward them just under the blue surface of the sea.

8

THE SUN WAS DEEP IN THE SKY, slipping into the darkening water, as dormant boats slowly began to wake. Ken moved to the railing and stood in silence, watching the channels gradually come to life with slow-moving traffic. To Adrienne everything seemed to be happening in slow motion. While the radio behind them was reporting devastating damage in the islands, Ken showed no sign of panic or willingness to rush, as if he still expected the alert to be a false alarm.

She joined him at the railing, and felt his arm move around her shoulder. The silent gesture made her feel protected, even in the blare of the doom-prophesying radio.

Tension around them was mounting; they could feel it and see it. A steady stream of boats now moved slowly past them: aristocratic, brass-fitted sailboats with naked masts; power-driven fishing vessels; yachts of varying sizes, varying ages. From the small channels, the boats converged to form a long convoy in the main channel of the harbor.

"We'd better go," he said softly.

A second after he said it, Harve Cooper called from across the catwalk, "When are you leaving?"

"About now!" Ken called back.

"Okay, that's what I was thinking—that we shouldn't wait any longer." He and another man, a stranger, stepped onto the catwalk. "We'll get these lines for you."

"Thanks." Ken moved toward the engine. "Adrienne, while they're untying us, can you unhook the shore power and water?"

When the *Firefly* was free of all her moorings, her engine began to roar like a tiger testing her freedom.

"You can sit in the captain's seat," he offered.

She paled. "I said I could steer, but I don't think I can maneuver us out of the slip without hitting something."

"I'll stand next to you and guide. Left-handed, without your help, I'd probably hit something, too, but the two of us can do it."

The channel behind them cleared temporarily when the Coopers vacated their slip. Activity on the deck of the cruiser on their starboard side and a wave from those at the rail indicated an intention to follow just behind the *Firefly*.

Ken worked the gears and gave short, specific directions to his pilot. She felt the power of an enormous engine beneath them as they backed slowly into the waterway. Had he not appeared so calm, she would have been extremely apprehensive about her ability to control his boat. If his composure was merely an act for her benefit, Adrienne thought, he was a very good actor.

"The tides are behaving strangely," Ken observed. "Look how the water has risen in the past thirty minutes. That's the first indication of seismic activity."

It was easy for her to steer the boat forward. As they chugged down the channel, she asked, "How do they predict the expected time of a hit?"

"Using principles of hydrodynamics. There's a tsunami warning system in Honolulu that's tapped into ocean-wide activity by computer."

"How high can seismic waves get?"

"I'm not sure. A hundred feet or higher."

"You're kidding!"

"No. A hundred-foot wave can flatten cities, but I don't think we need to anticipate anything that big."

"But it's possible?"

"With the ocean anything is possible. Seismic waves build as they travel. The shape of the ocean floor affects them, and as water depth decreases near shore, the bottom of the wave slows and the top rages shoreward."

Once out of the yacht basin, they were in the heavy harbor traffic. They joined commercial fishing boats, tour boats, U.S. Navy vessels—a moving fleet, all heading for the open sea. A city of boats was forming a mile or so off shore as dusk descended; lights began flicking on all around them. Behind were the first evening lights of San Diego and Point Loma.

Ken stood beside the raised captain's chair, letting her do most of the steering. He guided them past the congregation of boats and headed for deeper water. Adrienne was conscious of his shoulder pressing against hers.

"You're doing great," he said for the tenth time, but she wasn't certain whether to believe it. Whenever they veered close to another boat, and he had to reach for the wheel, she noticed the stain of perspiration under his arm. He was being especially nice, she thought, and she wondered how he decided when to be nice and when to be ornery. Maybe he was telling her he appreciated her help.

His closeness saturated her consciousness with the bold, rugged reality of him—of his male scent, of the movement of his broad chest as he breathed. An orange glow from the setting sun shone into the windshield, bathing his face with soft, amber light. The engine droned, nearly drowning out the radio voice reporting seismic activity all over the Pacific. Lights on the shore became more distant as the population of boats around them grew. A chill came from the sea. Adrienne was glad for the warmth of her sweat shirt.

"We'll keep going," he said. "We may as well get out of heavy traffic."

"Does my being at the helm worry you?"

"No. I'd just prefer to be out on the ocean alone with you."

She smiled. "What will happen when the wave gets here? Will we feel it?"

"I would think so. But I've never ridden a tidal wave before."

They drifted out to sea under stars. Ken said it would be a beautiful night for a sail, and lamented that he no longer owned his sailboat. She realized how little she knew about this man, who was beginning to occupy most of her waking and sleeping thoughts. He so seldom talked about himself.

"Your life has always been the ocean." It was a statement, rather than a question.

"Yeah. When I was in college I spent summers hiring out as a crew member for yachts sailing to the South Seas. I financed my education that way."

"You've sailed to Tahiti? Pago Pago?"

"Sure, all the way to Australia."

Adrienne saw something in his eyes sometimes—like now, when he looked at her a certain way that betrayed his thoughts. The thoughts were of her—his attraction to her. She saw it, felt it, trembled in vibrations of it. She couldn't understand why he was so reluctant to act on his feelings. He had never asked her for an actual date, not dinner or a walk along the beach. Intuition told her he preferred not to get romantically involved with her.

When they were a safe distance from other boats, Ken turned off the engine and they drifted. The silence, after the constant drone of the motor, brought the peace of the night to them.

"Why don't we get more comfortable?" he suggested, offering his one good arm to help her down from the captain's chair.

They sat on the fantail cushions, watching stars and the lights of moving boats on the water all around them, and listened for reports of the tidal wave on the radio. Ken excused himself after a time and went below, to reappear with two cans of beer precariously balanced in the sling.

She opened the beers and said, "Did you hear? Waves up to five feet were reported from San Diego a couple of minutes ago."

"It's beginning." He plopped down, ankle over knee, as if they were discussing baseball scores instead of a live tidal wave. She didn't have to see his eyes to know he was keeping a close watch on how they were drifting. The lights of one or two other vessels didn't look too far away.

She asked, "How long will we be out here?"

"Maybe all night," he said with a grin. "Our first night together. Which side of the bunk do you want?"

"You're a hundred percent bluff, Captain Burke. Or do you have a guardian angel to keep watch over the boat while we sleep?"

"Nope. I don't trust guardian angels. They play rotten tricks on me. Never be too trusting of angels. They'll get you every time."

"Is that where you learned your orneriness? From angels with little red horns?"

Ken sighed, sipping his beer. "Fate plays tricks on people, Adrienne."

She was unsure what he meant. "Was our meeting one of those tricks?"

He was awkwardly silent for a long time before he answered softly, "Yeah, I think so."

She blinked, stunned. "Why do you think so?"

"We're just..." He hesitated uncomfortably. "Just too damned different."

"You keep saying that. As if one of us were an alien. I'm not an alien, so it must be you."

"No, I'm human. Boy, am I ever human!"

His hand was touching her forearm, caressing lightly. He turned toward her and kissed her forehead, then her lips, lightly and deeply. Her head reeled; her stomach fluttered at the taste of him. Had they not been sitting down, she was certain she would have fallen, because her knees were becoming liquid, her self-control turning to vapor. How could a kiss do this? None ever had, before she'd met this man—this sorcerer. Through her sweat shirt, Adrienne could feel the rough textures of his sling and the hardness of the plaster cast.

"I'm human enough to want to feel your body close to me," he said as if he were reading her mind. "And all I can feel is this damned plaster."

"I know. Me, too. It's a convenient wall for you," she muttered as he held her.

"I don't want a wall between us."

"Are you sure?"

"I do want to be close to you," he asserted, his fingers brushing gently at her hair. " You're beautiful, Adrienne. It would be so easy to make love to you."

He actually said it! She pressed her hand to his cast, gazing hard at him. "Would it? With this encumbrance?"

His expression changed to one she had never seen— a glint of self-consciousness, of uncertainty, even unhappiness. He murmured, "Well, let's just say it's easy to think about." The fingers of his left hand fluttered over her face as if he were touching her for the first time. "I love to look at you, but every time I do, I get excited. And now, here beside you with the moon rising behind you, I want you in a way I've never...never..." He bent to her again, interrupting his own words with the press of his lips to hers.

Her heart pounded hard against her chest. Accepting his kiss was like rushing into a warm ocean. "Ken," she whispered, "is there any correlation between loving and wanting?"

"I don't know, Adrienne. I know very little about love."

His answer was truthful, at least. But he must have loved once. Perhaps he had even loved often. She didn't really know any more about love than he did, she mused. If she had ever really loved Richard, surely she wouldn't have forgotten him so quickly. And she didn't know if the fact that Ken made her feel things she'd never felt before meant she loved him, or if it was even possible to love a man she hardly knew.

Without warning, the *Firefly* lurched and rocked heavily. The lantern, which hung from a hook, swayed violently, sending snarled beams of light around their heads. The beer cans went sliding to the deck. Lights of the surrounding boats all rose in unison.

"Oh, Ken! The wave has gone under us!"

"No question about that," he said, reaching for the radio, which had slipped and tilted over in the swell. "She should be hitting the shore about now."

He turned up the volume. San Diego was reporting a hit—water rushing in for an estimated city block. As they listened, reports of the damage began coming in. Storefronts, small buildings, automobiles were pounded; there were threats to power lines. Strewn debris was everywhere as the water receded.

"Is that it, then?" Adrienne asked. "Is it over?"

"Oh, hell, no. There will be more waves. That one may have been just a baby. The night is far from over. We'll have to wait for an all clear." He turned down the volume. "Are you cold, Adrienne? There are jackets below in the forward locker. Maybe we ought to see what I have in the way of provisions."

Adrienne told him she would have a look, and then surprised him with a meal of spaghetti made from canned bacon-and-tomato sauce and canned mushrooms. They ate on the deck in dim yellow light, sharing a bottle of wine that Ken had brought out of storage. It was a cloudless night. A nearly full moon cast its glow over the water. Red, green and silver reflections from lights of drifting boats shone into the sea. Adrienne questioned him about dolphins. The more she learned, the more she found to ask. He was patient, teaching her.

Within the next four hours, three more tsunami hits were reported along the Pacific Coast. The second wave had barely begun to subside, when the third—and strongest, tore wildly at the beachfronts, crushing small buildings. Helicopter pilots continued to radio descriptions of the wave activity along the coast areas between Los Angeles and San Diego.

"They're estimating the waves at only six to eight feet," Adrienne said. "That doesn't sound so bad."

"It's misleading to call a seismic wave a wave at all, because waves rise up and down and peter out at the shoreline. A seismic wave is like a wall of water rampaging across the ocean at high speed and hitting any shore in its path at full force. A solid, rushing six-foot-high wall of water can do plenty of damage to shore areas. Bigger waves can move buildings."

"I'm glad we're out here, and not back in the harbor."

Ken grinned. "You're not one of those who wants to experience it first hand, huh? It must be an incredible sight. The wave sucks back and exposes the ocean floor before it rushes back to cover everything. I once heard of people in Hawaii running out on the reefs to pick up fish when the ocean sucked back just before the hit."

Adrienne's breath caught. "Ken! How could they?"

He shrugged. "Stupidity of the highest order. They didn't live to tell of their adventure."

"I'm surprised we didn't feel more turbulance at the top when the waves went under us. The ocean surface is unusually calm tonight, except for those three big swells, and they weren't so impressive, considering what they are."

"Eerie, isn't it?"

Far past midnight, when the wine was finished, Ken said to her, "You must be getting tired. I'll keep watch out here if you want to go below and sleep."

"I'll stay on deck with you. This may be the only tidal wave I ever ride."

"Having you here makes a long night seem short." He smiled, taking her hand.

When he kissed her, she snuggled against him, savoring the warmth of him, no longer feeling the night's chill.

ADRIENNE STOOD AT THE RAIL looking out at the yellow glow in the eastern sky behind the distant skyline of the city. The boats around them were becoming visible as the sunrise turned slowly into day. No seismic activity had been reported for more than four hours, and some of the boats had begun to creep shoreward. Ken started the engine and turned the *Firefly* toward the harbor entrance. Still no all clear had been given, but the boats and ships were restlessly churning the waters, bending the buoys, heading home. A few began drifting into the harbor channel, but it was another twenty minutes before the all clear sounded. Then Adrienne and Ken joined the caravan of heavy traffic. In so much congestion, it took concentration and cooperation at the wheel. As far as a mile out they saw debris from the destruction of the tidal waves. Floating logs and wood and unidentifiable flotsam and jetsam got thicker and thicker as they neared land. The ocean was muddy.

People stood at the boat rails, eager to get a look at the damage to the marina. Several of the dock-bound boats had been crushed under piers, but the piers, covered now with seaweed and debris, had held. The water was thick and brown and full of floating wood. A black-hulled ketch lay on her side, her mainmast torn away, heaving in the throbbing water like a dying animal. People were milling about, surveying damage, hauling capsized boats from the channels.

Other mariners, bleary eyed from the sleepless night, offered Ken help securing the *Firefly*'s moorings. The tide was so low he needed assistance to climb from deck to catwalk. By the time the craft was moored, rocking listlessly in the erratic tides, Adrienne was in the galley making coffee.

She handed the captain a steaming mug as he came below. He smiled and held up his cup in a salute. "The guy who said ships are safe in the harbor never saw a tidal wave. It's a mess out there."

She sat down, yawning, holding her cup in both hands.

"Sleepy, are you?"

"Why would I be sleepy just because we've been up all night?"

"It was a fine night, being with you, Adrienne. I'd be sorry it's over, except that now we can go to bed."

She looked at him through steam, over the top of her coffee mug. He slid off his jacket, which he had worn on only one arm, and gazed back at her. It was a tense moment, as if each expected the other to say something. But seconds passed and neither did, until he finally broke the gaze and set down the mug. He reached for her hand, a silent invitation.

She hesitated, studying his eyes, feeling tiredness ebb away in the wash of bold new vitality—anticipation and excitement blended. The boat seemed very small and private, a little world within itself—his world, into which he welcomed her. She accepted his hand and let him lead her in to the foreward cabin, his bedroom.

The room was larger than she had expected. It housed a double bunk, with shelves above, a dresser on one side and a wash basin with mirror on the other. The bed was spread with a heavy red fabric, and there were red curtains over the windows.

She asked, "Are you tired?"

"Tired? Nah, I'm a morning person. Sunrises are my source of energy. And today's sunrise was spectacular with the added beauty of your face. I'm too stimulated to be tired."

He sat on the edge of the bed, slid the sling from around his neck and tossed it onto the dresser. The cast was bent at the elbow, so he couldn't straighten his arm; its plaster extended up over his shoulder. Adeptly, well-practiced by now, he began to unbutton his shirt with his left hand.

Adrienne stood numbly, her arms at her sides, watching him, wondering what exactly he expected. Did he expect her to hurriedly get undressed, too? Without moving, she gazed at the curly hair on his chest, her heartbeat becoming erratic. For those few uncharted seconds, she was frightened of the part of Ken who was a stranger. She thought, *you never really know a man before you sleep with him. Gentleness can turn to lust without warning. Needing can turn into mechanics. Pure physical attraction can turn to shame—to doubts.*

Adrienne moved her eyes away, toward the closed red curtains, desperate with wanting him after the whole sleepless night of wanting him, but frightened because she didn't really know him.

His deep voice broke the silence. "What's the matter, Adrienne?"

"I'm not...sure...." It was part truth, part lie. Was it just the way he sat down and began so mechanically to undress—abruptly, without words? Was it the daylight at the windows, the sound of voices outside? *Was it fear that he was not what she dreamed he was?* Just because he sat on the bed and unbuttoned his shirt? She swallowed and avoided his eyes.

His hand reached out. His voice became so gentle it was almost a whisper. "Come here. Lie down beside me." Holding her, stroking her cheek, he whispered, "There's no reason to be afraid of me, Adrienne."

"I may be more afraid of myself than of you."

"Ah, that I understand. I'm afraid of myself, too— of my feelings...of wanting you more than I should. One part of me longs to be with you whenever I'm not. And the other part of me wants to go in the opposite direction, where I'm safe from your charms. You have a very disturbing effect on me, beautiful lady."

She smiled slowly, reassured by his soft voice, by the honesty in the confession of his own doubts. Inability to control feelings was something she had begun to experience since Ken. Now here he was, saying his feelings were no better under control than hers.

She touched his bare chest. "Do you sleep nude?"

"Doesn't everyone?"

"I don't."

"That's a shame. But any bad habit can be broken." He was kissing her forehead, then her cheeks.

"I like to sleep in satin."

"Umm," he murmured, his lips now on her neck. "You are satin."

His kisses cascaded down over her breasts, on the outside of her sweat shirt. Her breath quickened.

He mumbled, "Your spell is interfering with my best-laid plans. There's something I have to do."

"Now?"

"Soon."

She smiled. "You want to shower?"

"How did you know?"

"I've been sweating the night out, too. How do you keep your cast dry in the shower?"

"I have some plastic that fits over it, and one of those hand shower heads. It's a crude operation, which I could manage better if the stall weren't so damned small. Unfortunately there's no room for two people to shower at once. I wish there were. Do you want a turn first?"

She scooted to the head of the bed and propped herself against his pillows. "No. I don't mind being second. Go right ahead."

" A proper host wouldn't go first."

She smiled mischievously and raised one knee, resting her arm against it, watching him through half-squinting eyes that she hoped did not reveal the wild excitement rising in her, the wild anticipation of finding out for herself if he had been teasing about the underwear. "I insist!"

He returned her smile with a shrug and bent over to take off his deck shoes and socks. Then he stood up, fumbling with the top button of his jeans. He pulled the tight pants down slowly, shifting his left hand from one side to the other until the jeans were loose enough for him to kick free. He stood almost still for several seconds, naked, legs apart, saying nothing, just inviting her to look at him. She did unashamedly, stunned by the beauty of his body. The change of skin color where his tan stopped was in bands of various shades, tan lines from several different swimsuits.

"It wouldn't do me much good now to deny how much I want you, would it?"

She shook her head, tingling with arousal at the sight of his. No, he could not deny his!

He wrapped a clear plastic material over his cast, while she watched mutely, having lost most of her voice. Too soon he disappeared behind the narrow door of his shower stall, and she heard the splashing water.

Adrienne took off her shoes and stretched out on his bunk, knowing Ken was anticipating her turn next. A delicious, tantalizing game! She slid her sweat shirt over her head, took off her jeans and was sitting in her underwear, when he emerged, dripping, drying his hair.

"Invigorating!" he said, and only then did Adrienne remember that the boat had no hot water. She had never taken a cold shower in her life, and the thought was not a pleasant one. But since she had not showered since yesterday morning, there wasn't much choice.

It seemed tragic to have to take her eyes from Ken's naked body—to have to ever take her eyes from the sight of him—tall, powerfully muscled and...wanting her, even after a cold shower! She rose from the bed, watching Ken dry himself hurriedly and toss off the plastic cover from his cast. With the towel over his shoulders, he embraced her, feeling hard and wet and cold against her. When he kissed her, small beads of water from his thick, damp hair trickled onto her forehead. He smelled clean and soapy. Her body burned hot against his cool skin.

With his thumb and forefinger he was able to unhook her bra. His embrace lightened as he stepped back to slide the straps from her shoulder, freeing her pale breasts, gazing down at them with approving eyes. "So lovely."

His caresses were a thirsty breeze of spring, building to announce a coming storm. They moved over her breasts, down over the small of her back, then her stomach, until his fingers caught the elastic of her panties—an almost transparent little garment of lace. He knelt on one knee and slid the lace gently away, pressing small kisses to her stomach, touching her lightly with his fingertips. She felt the mat of his damp hair against her heated body before he stood again and gazed down at her with strange, half-misting eyes. His breathing was heavy. She could not hear the heaving of his chest, but she could feel it.

She asked, "Is it terribly cold?"

"Not anymore."

"I meant the shower."

"I missed you in the shower. I don't want us to be parted again."

"I'll hurry, I promise."

"The water's cold," he warned, brushing his lips over her breasts.

"It will be the fastest shower on record."

It was. And it was hard to keep from squealing at the shock of the cold water. How could he stand to live this way, in such tiny quarters with so few possessions, without even the small luxury of hot water?

He had removed the red bedspread and was lying on the sheet when she opened the shower door; his naked body looked very dark against the white.

"Cold?"

She nodded, shivering, drying her face. Her blond hair, which she had tried to keep from getting soaked in the shower, curled damply in ringlets around her forehead.

"Come on. I'll dry you. And warm you."

She curled next to him and let him dry her by teasing the towel all over her body. Then he tossed it across the room and pulled her against him, pressing his parted lips to hers, smoothing his tongue over her teeth and her tongue. She moved her knee slowly up over him, feeling his hardness against her thigh. Wriggling closer, she rubbed her thigh sensually over him and made him moan.

Adrienne closed her eyes in submission to his tender touch as she felt his hand slide over her body. Only one hand, drawing her into surrender. God, what could he do with two?

He whispered her name with his breath quivering over her, his lips rippling over her. Over her breasts, her stomach, the soft insides of her thighs. His breath asking, promising.

"So lovely..." she heard him whisper, his voice rasping and full.

He reached the essence of her being, physically and emotionally. She shuddered violently and grabbed at his shoulders. "Ken..." she breathed, unable to lie still under his touch.

"Too much?"

"Oh...I don't know...too soon." She squirmed. "You're making me...crazy."

"Let it happen," he whispered. "Let me..."

Warmth of his lips, electrifying shocks surging through her. Loss of breath, almost of consciousness for wild, uncountable seconds. She gasped, "How do you know...so well...?"

"I let you tell me, in your silent way."

"And you—will you tell me?"

"Yes." He turned onto his back and began to guide her hand gently. "Yes, I'll tell you...here."

He groaned as her fingers curled over him, fingers wakening to his strength and to his vulnerability all at once, seeking his armor only to disarm. Rich circles of love seeking the core of his manhood, to fulfill a promise and, for the moment, to possess. To consume.

Adrienne trembled, lost in the passionate spring of promise that Ken's warm body offered her. This was desire with more aching than she had ever imagined. This was longing to be closer to this man than it was possible to be.

Except one way. She said his name. His hand found the softness of her breasts again. His voice was rasping. "I can't wait...any longer."

"Don't wait!"

He twisted, fighting the weight of his cast, and grunted as he rolled over. Perspiration shone on his skin. She hadn't thought very much about the restrictions of the cast until this moment, but it didn't matter now. Nothing mattered but being close to him, being part of him, to accept the power and the strength and the primal essence of him!

She touched the cast and looked into his eyes as he moved over her. Lowering himself to her, he held her misty blue gaze. Locked deep in an image of love was the indelible coupling of spirit to spirit, of flesh to flesh.

Adrienne held on to him, clasping his body to hers, joining in the ebb and flow of the eternal rhythm. Rhythm like the tides—washing, building, crashing! Crashing....

The wave swept over her, drowning her in its fiery heat, filling her, flooding her with the strangest sensation of joy she had ever known.

"My love..." Ken breathed without a voice before the spasm overtook him, before the arm supporting all his weight gave way to the heavy, trembling fragments of release.

With a cry, shaking violently, he fell heavily against her. Adrienne grunted and fought for her breath, but several seconds passed and Ken lay still, his face close to hers, his breaths coming in great gasps. Still trembling, hurting under his weight, she waited.

He seemed to have to fight for strength to lift himself. She felt the scraping of the plaster against her breast as he rolled sideways, grunting an apology.

"I'm sorry. My wrist is still sore and couldn't hold me any longer. Did I hurt you?"

She saw worry in his eyes. Her only answer was a kiss brushed against his eyelids, then his lips.

He shifted closer to her, trying to find a comfortable position, still breathing hard. "Are you all right?"

"Yes. Are you?"

"This moment, never better! But suddenly I can feel fatigue from a night without sleep. Will you stay and sleep with me? Is there something you have to get home for this morning?"

"I'm too tired to remember."

Grunting with effort, Ken raised himself up to reach the edge of the sheet. He pulled it over them, rolling sleepily onto his back. With eyes closed, he mumbled, "You're beautiful...beautiful." A deep, shaky sigh. "Adrienne, I always meant to ask you..." His voice faded into the hollow, musty silence of the softly swaying boat.

"Ask me what?"

"Umm...never mind...I'll ask you when I wake up."

She lay for some minutes, watching Ken sleep. The cabin was warming with morning sun. Water lapped lazily at the hull; the boat rocked like a cradle, creaking as it pulled at its moorings. A new happiness flooded Adrienne like music. If her spirit were to be trapped in this moment forever, then this new, melodic gypsy music would be forever part of her. So this was how it really felt to be in love!

9

THROUGH AN OPEN WINDOW a breeze teased the short, sun-faded curtains. Adrienne lay in the gentle rocking of the boat, watching the lazy flapping of red fabric at the window and listening to the soft rhythm of Ken's breathing. The ocean air outside was alive with voices of people still busy clearing away debris from last night's tidal wave. The sounds of the harbor would not wake Ken; he was used to them and to the rocking. A slant of sunlight streaked across the bed, over his chest, sparking against the white cast.

Eventually he stirred; his eyes fluttered open and he smiled sleepily. "What time is it?"

"Around ten o'clock, I think."

"Did I dream it, or did the planet soar out of its orbit this morning?"

She smiled dreamily, ruffling the curly hair that fell over his forehead. "I think the planet is still out of orbit. Everything looks new, even the sun."

His hand moved to her breast and caressed lovingly. Knowing moving wasn't easy for him, she bent toward him—an offering to his lips.

"You taste so good," he mumbled, accepting. "My hunger is insatiable."

The moist exploration of his tongue over her breasts brought back the morning's music. Ken kicked the sheet away from their bodies, exposing his eager, masculine passion.

"I was lying here burning to touch you," she confessed.

"Why didn't you?"

"You were sleeping so peacefully."

"Dreaming you were touching me. . .umm. . .like now. . .like that."

She shifted down. "Ken, do you want. . .?"

His fingers twisted heavily through her hair as he spoke in a hard, rasping whisper. "Yes. . .yes, I want. . .want you to. . ."

To take his throbbing warmth and make it part of her!

To taste his storming passion!

To give, to take, not knowing which was giving and which was taking!

His thighs quivered. She felt his shiver blend with hers. Heard him breathe her name to plead for less. . .and more. . . .

Adrienne rose slowly, breathing hard, and straddled him, gazing down at him. The magic lit his face; the passion glazed his eyes. She leaned to kiss him.

"We must give your sprained wrist a rest," she said, rocking forward and then back, over him, easing herself down slowly.

He moaned, closing his eyes.

She sought and found the rhythm of the tides again, sought and found the exquisite love-agony in his handsome face, submission to a power greater than his own. Submission to the unrestrained thrusts of her love for him.

"TELL ME ABOUT YOU," he said later, as they lay in bed, not wanting anything more of the morning than each other. "Why did you come to California?"

"I thought I told you."

"You left out too much. I had the feeling you were running from a love affair, something like that."

"I recently terminated a love affair, but it wasn't the reason I left New York."

"Your cousin said you lived in Boston."

"My home is Boston. I've been studying at the Manhattan Music Institute for the past three years, working toward a doctorate.

"That's very impressive. So why did you come West?"

"To visit Carmen and my Aunt Hester, as I said."

"Yes, that's what you said. But you took the job at the Sea Cliff."

"I wasn't ready to go home, because I hadn't..." Adrienne paused. The memory of the last awful conversation with Richard slammed at her head. She shook it away. How could she tell this man beside her now—the man she knew she loved—that she didn't have the slightest notion who she was? How do you explain that your whole identity is a forgery? None of that nightmare had anything to do with Ken. He accepted her for the person he perceived her to be—just herself. Not the Canaday heiress, not a nameless orphan. Just herself. At least for now, that meant everything to her. There was no reason for Ken to know about her frustrating quest for her identity or for the sordid, long-buried reasons behind all the illegalities her mother had perpetuated just to keep her. No, her identity problem was too private to share with him, until she had some answers.

She began again. "I was very close to my mother. I miss her. And I'm renewing a childhood friendship with Carmen. California is a more comfortable place for me right now."

"But you'll return to New York?"

"Yes, probably in the fall."

Ken's eyes left her. He watched the curtains flapping gently in a square of sunlight. "I may go to Australia in the fall. The lab may be closed by then, and I'll have to continue my work in Melbourne."

"I had no idea you were thinking of closing the lab."

"We hope we won't have to. It depends on several things, none of which makes for interesting conversation."

She sighed deeply, feeling emptiness at the thought of such a parting. "I want to know more about you, Ken."

"Well, I have a son. He lives in the San Fernando Valley with his mother and a stepfather who is a better father than I am. Jeff's a great kid. He's the main reason I'd hate like hell to have to move to Australia. When we do see each other..." His voice dropped away.

Because of the sadness in his eyes, Adrienne would not ask any more about Ken's son. She smiled. "You've been a bachelor for several years. You must like it."

He frowned. "I don't know if I like it or dislike it. It's just the way I have to live."

"*Have* to?"

"Yes." His eyes were serious as they glanced away and back to her. "My life-style is pretty austere, don't you think? No woman on earth is crazy enough to want to live the way I do. Once I had to choose between my job and my marriage, and though I cringe sometimes to admit it, I chose the job. I'd do it again. My work is an obsession."

He sighed. "I wish you wouldn't look at me like that, Adrienne. I know what you're thinking. But it wasn't my idea to get married. We were kids. I was busy sailing boats around the Pacific. My girlfriend deliberately got pregnant between trips because she knew it was the only way I'd ever agree to marriage. Resentment over that didn't help our chances much, either. But mostly it was my lack of money. There are no financial rewards in this kind of research. It's nothing but a struggle. I just have nothing. . .nothing to give a woman."

She studied him. "One has to be obsessed to give one's life to something the way you have to the dolphin research."

"Yeah. No question about it."

"I've heard some gossip about you, though. I've heard there are scores of women who would kill to be introduced to you."

He grinned. "That's bull."

"Not from what I hear."

"There isn't one score of women who even know I'm alive. I haven't been to a party in two years. I drive an old pickup, live on an old boat, and nearly every dime I make from my books goes back into the lab. No California playboy has any competition from me." He smiled and touched her bare shoulder gently, ran his fingers down her arm and brushed a kiss across the scars on her hand. "After all, it took a tidal wave to get us together."

"I've been thinking about that." *Please don't ask about the scars*, she begged silently as his kiss lingered on her hand.

"You're a good sailor, Adrienne, among other things. You've been around boats."

"Yes, but I had to overcome a childhood fear of them, like my fear of water. I must have come into the world with an oversupply of phobias. My mother was very understanding and did everything to help me conquer my fears."

"Nobody comes into the world with built-in phobias," he said. "If you were afraid of boats and water, there must have been some reason. Something frightened you. Your mother must have known what it was."

Adrienne wondered. After all, her mother hadn't even known her name. She shivered, wanting the joys of this morning with Ken to blot out the disturbances of her shadowy past. "Well, you were frightened of marriage. Is that a phobia now?"

He smiled. "Yeah, I think so. Something like that."

"You really wouldn't marry again? Ever?"

"No. It wouldn't work for me."

"What if you fell in love?"

"I wish I were immune to love, Adrienne. It would make my life a lot simpler. But I'm not immune to human needs and passions. I just have to give the command of my life to my head, not my heart. My head rules without mercy and won't ever get me into another jam. Marriage just isn't for me."

"What do you want," she asked in a husky voice, "from me?"

Several tense seconds preceded his soft answer. "That friendship you offered me. Some sharing, like we've had. If you stay in California and want to continue spending time with the dolphins, we could share that, too. I thought at first we couldn't be friends because of the strong physical attraction between us that was obvious from the day we met. But you've shown me it could work, because of our common interests and because we have compatible personalities. I like being with you. Last night, and especially this morning, have meant a lot to me."

"To me, too," she confessed, while a voice inside her goaded, *but how do I get over this now? How do I get over you?*

AUNT HESTER STOOD ON THE LANDING, making high-pitched cries of protest. "You'll kill yourselves! You'll break your backs with that trunk!"

"We've almost got it, Mother," Carmen grunted. "Okay, Adrienne, next step! Easy does it!"

The hulking old steamer trunk balanced grudgingly against their backs as it slid down the carpeted stairs. They were creeping down one step at a time, allowing the trunk to follow with heavy thuds.

"You'll never get that thing back up the stairs," Hester complained. "Does it have to be down here?"

"It's all papers, Mom. It will take hours to go through it and the light in the attic isn't good enough. The trunk won't be in your way in the spare room."

Hester smiled with a shrug. "It's worth all this if you find anything, but I can't imagine what that might be."

"A clue to Adrienne's secret past. Maybe a ring with the seal of British royalty! Or a sealed document proving she's the illegitimate daughter of an exiled Russian count with whom her mother had a whirlwind affair."

"Or a paid-in-full receipt from a baby smuggler in Algiers," Adrienne snorted.

The trunk bounced safely over the last step and onto the upstairs landing. "Third door down the hall," Carmen directed. "Let's get behind this clumsy monster and push him the rest of the way."

Hester watched the slow trek over her thick carpet with skepticism. But patience paid off. In the spare bedroom, cheering over their victory and panting heavily, Carmen plopped down on top of the trunk. "This thing must weigh three hundred pounds! How could daddy collect so much junk in only one lifetime?"

Adrienne dropped to the floor exhausted. "Aunt Hester's right. We'll never get this back up the stairs."

"One challenge at a time. For now, let's organize this job. We need music and something smashing to drink. What's appropriate background music for this be-ghosted venture into your unknown? Tchaikovsky? Rimski-Korsakov? Yes, good! Something Russian. Then, of course, we'll need vodka." She snapped her fingers. "Screwdrivers!"

"What's this about Russian? I've no reason to suspect I'm Russian!"

"I know, but it's the perfect background for intrigue. I tantalized myself with my exiled-Russian-count theory. One of the world's least known facts is that six Russians in ten, given the choice, prefer American women. So—"

"Now wait a minute, Carmen! How could you possibly know a thing like that? You've always had a terrific memory, I'll admit, but you'd have to have a photographic memory and an abnormal fetish for trivia to memorize so many oddball statistics. Six Russians in ten prefer American women. Come on!"

Carmen laughed, brushing a lock of dark hair from her eyes. "Of course I don't memorize statistics! What kind of idiot do you take me for? I just make them up."

"You do? All of them?"

"Well, sure! I learned a long time ago that people never argue with statistics. So I make up statistics to fit the occasion."

Adrienne dissolved in laughter. "I'm stunned at such shocking deceit!"

"It's all for a good cause."

"What cause?"

"Me! Ninety-nine times out of a hundred I win my point!"

"I think I could learn a lot from you," Adrienne said with a laugh. "If I could sort out fact from fiction."

Ten minutes later, braced with Rimski-Korsakov and a pitcher full of screwdrivers, they opened the lid of the big black trunk, and wheezed at the volume of papers and boxes before them. In old shirts streaked with attic dust, they settled down on the floor and began to make stacks.

"What are we looking for?" Carmen asked.

"I have no idea. Any kind of birth document, immigration papers, letters. Anything to do with a baby."

Humming the melodious "Song of India," Carmen leaned back against the trunk with a pile of papers in her hand. "You're sleeping with Kendall Burke, aren't you?"

Adrienne didn't look at her cousin. "What brought on that question so suddenly?"

"Nothing sudden. I've been dying to ask for two days. You were with him all Sunday night on his boat."

"We were drifting around on top of a tidal wave with a thousand other boats. We talked all night and kept watch and listened to the radio."

"Okay, I'll buy that. You spent the night getting..." Carmen's eyebrow raised with her smirk before she cleared her throat. "Getting, shall we say, worked up to x-rated imagery? Then what happened the next morning?" She slapped the thick blue carpet with her hand. "Aha! there's a genuine blush! You did sleep together! I knew it! You lucky dog! Is it possible to sleep with that guy without falling in love with him?"

Adrienne was sullen for a time, sipping, sorting through papers. She finally answered, "I doubt it."

Carmen grinned evilly. "Richard has lost you for good, the stupid snob! Is Kendall in love with you?"

"Kendall is in love with dolphins. The only lasting relationship he wants is with them."

"No man ever knows what he really wants. It's up to us to tell them."

Adrienne groaned. "This man does. He lives without hot water."

"What does that mean? That he prefers cold showers to a warm body? Even you wouldn't believe that story, Adrienne."

She chuckled. "It means he literally has no hot water. He lives with barely the basic human necessities, cramped up on that old boat. His closet hardly has anything in it. The guy has real hermit tendencies."

"I don't want to hear all that background stuff. I want to know what it was like making love with him!"

"I can't tell you because there is nothing to compare it to. One wouldn't expect him to have such a gentle touch, but he does. Even with the cast..."

"Oh, no! I forgot about the cast! How did he...?"

"Never mind how. He's a man of great ingenuity."

"That figures. And vast experience."

In her mind, Adrienne could feel the constant rocking, hear the creaking sounds of the boat, see the master cabin once again and the rumpled bed, smell the soapy scent of Ken's naked body next to her, hear his cry of surrender...such temporary surrender. She lowered her head and tried to force back an overpowering sense of loss.

"Hey! What's wrong? Hey, are you crying?"

Adrienne sniffed. "You make so light of everything, Carmen. I can't make light of this with Ken. My feelings are too strong. I got myself into this before I realized what I was doing. Walked right into it! And now that I'm hopelessly in love, how do I get out, short of dying?"

"Why do you have to get out? Just because he lives without hot water..."

"He's been honest with me about his feelings. He likes me as a friend—oh, sure, as a lover, too, but he doesn't want a woman in his life. He'll never marry."

"Yipes! There's that word again! Of course, you'd never marry him, so what's—"

"Why wouldn't I?"

Carmen stared, too stunned to comment.

Adrienne thumbed through a few papers before she looked at her cousin again. "All my values have changed since I met Ken and the dolphins. I feel really alive for the first time in my life. But for Ken, our friendship is only temporary. He gives himself completely to his research—all his energy, love, money. There's nothing left for anything else."

"The money part doesn't matter. You have enough for both."

"He doesn't know that."

Carmen's face darkened. "Are you sure?"

"Of course I'm sure. I've never told him about...any of my past."

"He may know about the money, though, since his buddy Brian knows."

"How could he? Oh! Damn you, Carmen!"

"Well! Did I know you were playing Cinderella? Besides, I was smashed that night."

"No wonder Ken keeps making remarks about how opposite we are and how I'm used to the finer things in life."

"Well, you are!"

"The finest thing in my life is what Ken and I had last weekend. And I'm not used to it. I'd better not get used to it either unless I intend to die an early death from heartbreak."

Carmen fell into silence.

"You didn't tell him about all this legal mess with my adoption, did you?"

"No. I know you're sensitive about all that."

Music and the shuffling of papers filled the room. After a time, Adrienne said, "These are all just insurance policies, deeds, receipts, and personal stuff of your dad's."

"Boring, isn't it? But we got this trunk down here, so let's make sure we comb through it."

After two hours they were on their second pitcher of drinks and the Rimski-Korsakov had been replaced by jazz. Carmen was on her stomach on the floor, balanced on one elbow, searching through a shoe box.

"Here are some of dad's passports."

"Let's see those."

Adrienne sorted through the thin green books, remembering her Uncle Raleigh as a much older man than the man in the photos. She could arrange the books in sequence by the photographs, each face older than the one before.

"Here's something interesting!" She sat up, holding a book away from the others. "One of mother's passports is in here! Why would that be? This looks like a duplicate of one I have—same photograph!"

Her trembling fingers began leafing through the document, studying each page.

Carmen set down her drink and scooted closer. "What are you looking for?"

"I'm looking at the stamps to see if they're different—they are different! Look, Carmen! This stamp—'RSA Binnekoms-Entry'—is the same as the one in the passport I have, but the date is different!"

"Are you sure?"

"Absolutely. I've memorized all the stamps by now. My passport, which is a forgery, has stamps of Europe all over it, and all match stamps on mother's passport and on this passport, as near as I can determine so far—except this one."

"'RSA?'" Carmen's nose wrinkled. "Where's that?"

"The Republic of South Africa. That must mean mother was there twice."

"So? Laura traveled a lot..."

"One of these two passports is also a forgery, Carmen, don't you see? And it must be the other one, the one which has the later of these two RSA stamps. Mother didn't want it to show she had been there before she was there with me! Hester is certain she brought me from somewhere overseas. It could have been from there."

"Africa?" Carmen muttered. "*Africa?* You think your mother brought you from *there*?"

"It kind of looks that way."

"There's something in that passport, Adrienne—a paper."

Two small, faded slips of paper fell from the book. Adrienne straightened as she opened them with trembling fingers.

"Hey, look at this! One is a hotel receipt and the other looks like it might be a car-rental receipt!" She smoothed the wrinkles in the thin paper. "Hotel Ngukwelena, Julius Bay. Where in the world is Julius Bay?"

"It shouldn't be too hard to find out. And when we do, what then? From the sound of that name, cuz, I don't think the place is in France or England."

"It's in South Africa—I'd bet on it. And if it is, then I'm going there to check it out."

"You can't! It's...it's just a wild-goose chase! The wildest of goose chases!"

"I don't think so. Look at it logically. The only reason mother would have tampered with her own passport would have been because of my fake passport. Wherever this place is, it sounds pretty remote, doesn't it? Why would mother go twice to a place like that?"

"You don't know that she—"

"Here's the date on the hotel receipt! One day after the entry date that's on my passport! So there is a connection! There is!"

Carmen sighed heavily as she drained her glass. "Okay, cuz, suppose this does show your mother was at that hotel with you? Do you really think traveling all the way to—"

"This must be the place! Why else would this passport and the receipt be with your dad's stuff?" She stood up, twirling and hugging the green document to her chest. "I think we've found it, Carmen!"

Her cousin scowled. "Who would have guessed Africa, with your complexion?"

"This was a lucky find! Thank heavens you have your father's things, or we might never—"

"I'll go with you," Carmen interrupted.

"I'd rather go alone. It's something I really want to do alone."

"You don't even know where Julius Bay is!"

"I've traveled all my life. I enjoy it. It doesn't matter where it is."

"We need another drink!" Carmen decided, clinking the ice in her empty glass. We need a drink and an Atlas and smelling salts for when we drop this bomb on mother!"

THREE DAYS LATER, as the first light of morning touched the white curtains of the east windows, Adrienne lay with Ken on rumpled sheets in his small apartment at the lab.

He was smiling at her. "You didn't sleep very well. You were tossing and mumbling."

"You didn't sleep well, either. Several times when I woke, you were groaning as if you were in pain."

"The cast is uncomfortable. I'm sick to death of it. I'm nurturing explicit fantasies of how I'm going to make love to you without it."

She felt his thigh move against her, felt the heave of his sighing chest against her, felt the warmth of his hand exploring her.

"You make waking up a special occasion," he whispered.

"We must be careful not to get too used to it."

"Why? Every morning I wake with you beside me will always be special."

She nodded. "Special, but addictive. There is always a price to pay for addiction."

"Yes, my love. Yes, I know."

His tender caressing searched for and received her response. Passion rose in her. She reached to him, wanting him—so desperately wanting him. Not just this moment, this morning, but all mornings, forever.

"Ken...it hurts to want you so much."

"I know the feeling." He kissed her. "But we know how to make it better."

Yes, make it better, her heart said. *Make love to me and the world will go away.* But, no, this morning she had to deal with reality first. "Ken, what's going to become of us?"

"You mean in the future?"

She nodded.

A glimmer of hurt shone in his eyes. "I haven't allowed myself to think about it. I suppose you'll return to New York and become a famous concert pianist, and I'll stand in line for your autograph."

"But not in New York, I'll bet."

"We'll get together. We'll make a point of it. If you don't forget me in the glitter of a celebrity's life."

"Being a celebrity isn't important to me. It never has been."

"It isn't?" He seemed surprised. "What is important to you?"

"The dolphins are." Words caught huskily in her throat. "And you are."

The hurt in his eyes deepened, and he frowned. "The dolphins and I are a chapter in what promises to be an extraordinary life. You have the world at your feet, my love. You've such a fascination for everything around you, such a capacity to make every experience rich and exciting. I'm glad I can be a little part of all that, maybe even a special part. But later, while I'm struggling along at my snail's pace, you'll be conquering the earth."

You don't know me, she thought. But, then, how could he? She'd only just come to know herself, to know what really mattered to her. And even were she not powerless to make him believe that, even if she could make him understand, Adrienne didn't know if it would change anything.

She lifted her hand from his shoulder. "You asked what was important to me and I told you. And then you proceeded to tell me what's important to me. And they're not the same."

He looked startled. "I didn't want to hear you say I'm important to you. It isn't fair to either of us, but mostly to you. You're too good for me and we both know it."

"'Too good'? That's stupid!" She tried to calm her voice. "Am I not important to you?"

"Of course you're important to me! But I...but you said..."

"I know what I said. You're worried that it came out sounding as if I meant I'm in love with you and that I'd rather stay with you than play the piano."

His circling fingers had moved to her back now, brushing tenderly over her skin. His voice became barely audible. "You didn't mean it that way, did you?"

"Yes. I did."

The hurt in his eyes darkened to pain and the caressing ceased. "Adrienne, look at your life and mine! You've so much to look forward to. You can go anywhere, be anything. You're an aristocrat with aristocratic tastes."

"Stop telling me what I am, Ken! Or what I feel! You can't get inside me. You don't know how I feel! What makes you such an expert on me, anyhow? You don't even know me!" Angry, she sat up in the bed, pulling the sheet over her breasts.

He raised himself on his elbow and stared at the grip of anger on her face. "I'm only trying to protect you."

"No, you're trying to protect yourself. You and your unshakable ideas."

"Now you're telling me what I feel. I have damn good reasons for my convictions."

"Sure. Based on what you think I am, not what I really am!" Her tear-filled eyes darted away from him and to the ceiling.

"Hell, I've tried to be as up-front as I could."

"I guess you have," she conceded, lowering her head into her arms in a gesture of shame and surrender. "You tried to keep everything light. It's not your fault I'm such a fool. I was trying to tell you how I feel before I go, on the one shot in a billion you might understand."

"Before you go where? I thought you were staying to work with Aphrodite this morning."

"I can't. I have a plane to catch."

His thick eyebrows arched. "For where? Are you going home?"

"No, I'm going to Africa."

"'Africa'? Just like that? Without saying anything? Why are you suddenly going to Africa?"

"It has to do with...well, it's family business."

The line of his mouth tightened. "Are you coming back?"

"To California? I'm not sure. I'm really not sure, Ken." She turned, but she knew it was not in time to hide the fear in her eyes from him. How could she explain that everything—even whether she returned to San Diego—could depend on what she found in Africa? She couldn't explain; she couldn't even try.

For what seemed an eternity, Ken didn't speak. He wasn't even looking at her now; his eyes were fixed on some invisible point on the wall across the room. She was forcing back tears. There would be time later for tears. She already felt enough of a fool.

At length his dark, husky voice said, "I'll miss you."

"I'll miss you, too."

"I didn't figure on...on your leaving so soon."

"I hate to leave the work with Aphrodite. But I have to do this...."

"Halfway around the world, Adrienne? Why? To get away from me?"

"No, but I do have to get away from you. It's best for me."

"Maybe it's best for both of us, but I don't like it."

"Staying will only make me love you more, and you've been clear on your opinion about any woman who would do such a stupid thing as love you."

He sighed. "You wouldn't be able to stand life with me. I know. I've been through the kind of frustration it would mean for both of us—your discomfort and my guilt for all the things I could never give you."

"Now you're starting it again! Why do you insist on telling me what would make me happy or unhappy? You think you know me, but you don't. The wall you've built between us isn't even there, except in your mind." She bit her lip in an oppressive haze of frustration. "I could never even convince you how much your dolphins mean to me, could I?"

"No, my love," he answered softly. "No, you never could."

10

HOTEL NGUKWELENA SHOWED ITS AGE. The only two-story building in the sleepy town of Julius Bay on the Transkei's Wild Coast, its windows were permanently clouded by salt-moist winds. Dank ocean smells permeated the floorboards of its railed porch. On the ground floor, the lobby opened to a small dining room that served as a tearoom every afternoon.

Pale-pink tablecloths were faded from countless washings. Plaster cracked and peeled on shell-pink walls. White curtains, woven through with age-frayed silver threads, frizzed in the light of late-afternoon sun. Wood floors were polished to a sheen. Adrienne sipped her tea and gazed out the window at a blue-white winter sky above a little walled garden—the Southern Hemisphere's winter in July. She was trying to imagine her mother being here, in this same room, twenty-four years earlier. Laura Canaday might have been wearing white that day. She wore white often. Her hair would have been dark then, like Hester's and Carmen's, and it might have been tucked under one of those little brimmed hats she loved.

It was true that Laura Canaday had been drawn to quaint, out-of-the-way places in her extensive travels, but this dot on the globe was less quaint than simply poor, and not Laura's sort of haunt at all. Farther down

the coast highway toward the Cape were resorts with
fine beaches, magnificent scenery and adequate ho-
tels. But Julius Bay was an insignificant fishing village
on the Wild Coast, where tourists seldom stopped. Except for the hotel proprietor, who looked to be East Indian, every person she had seen was African.

Adrienne was the only customer in the tearoom this
late afternoon. Restlessly she watched the door until the
proprietor, a man in his early forties, stepped through
the double doors from the lobby.

"I'm sorry I kept you waiting, madam. I was told you
wanted to talk to me."

"Yes." She smiled up at him and motioned to the opposite chair. "Do you have a few minutes? Won't you
sit down?"

His dark eyes squinted in confusion.

Adrienne understood his hesitancy to sit with her.
"I'm American. I don't know or care about the rules of
social protocol here. I have something I'd like to show
you, if you wouldn't mind."

The man pulled out the chair slowly and sat down.
"Certainly."

She reached into her shoulder bag for an envelope,
from which she produced two green passport books
and some photos. "I believe my mother stayed at this
hotel twenty-four years ago. I don't suppose you were
here then."

"No, I came from Natal eight years ago."

"I realize twenty-four years is a long time, but do you
know anyone who might possibly remember? Anyone
who might have met my mother? I'm trying to retrace
her steps to find out why she came to Julius Bay. It's very
important to me."

She received a wide friendly smile, a tilt of shiny black hair toward her. "Samuel has been here longer than anyone else I know."

"Samuel? Does he work here?"

"Yes, at the hotel. He's a religious leader of sorts, and I'm told there is little that goes on in the village that he doesn't know about. Samuel speaks no English, but he is the only person I can think of who might be of help."

"Would he be willing to talk to me? Could you interpret?"

"Certainly. Samuel is a very friendly man, a Christian man." He rose from the table. "I saw him a few minutes ago. If you want to wait in the garden, I'll find him just now."

The little garden was adorned with sparse clusters of winter flowers. A white wooden bench sat under an acacia tree on pale-green grass. From the top of the wall, a chorus of little brown birds was chirping. Adrienne, pacing a narrow stone path, could feel the first chill of early dusk.

Within minutes, the hotel proprietor returned in the company of an old man with white hair and black skin. Samuel, dressed neatly in a black shirt and black pants, smiled at her and gave a little bow of his head. In spite of his age, his teeth were white and gleaming.

She showed him the pictures of her mother and of her at the age of two, and stood breathless, her eyes darting to the interpreter and back to the old man, waiting for his response. It came in the form of a broad smile, a blink of shining black eyes and excited words in an unfamiliar language.

"Samuel remembers your mother," the interpreter said. "She was here twice."

"He remembers? He's certain?"

The old man held the picture of Laura Canaday in front of him, pointing, and nodding to Adrienne with a smile, communicating recognition without benefit of language. His meaning was clear. He did remember!

She smiled back, unable to conceal her rising excitement. Sharing the excitement, Samuel began to chatter rapidly.

The hotel proprietor translated, "The madam in this photo was here first with two other ladies who spoke a European language Samuel had never heard. He believes it was perhaps French. The second time the lady visited the hotel she was alone."

With the old man nodding enthusiastically, Adrienne's heart had begun to pound wildly. He was correct—she was certain! The women would be the DuVeaux sisters, Laura's lifelong friends from Paris, with whom she often traveled. Whether or not it was miraculous that the old man would remember three well-dressed European women, the important thing was, he did remember!

Adrienne's voice almost stuck in her throat as she posed the next question. She pointed to her own photograph. "Ask Samuel if he ever saw this little girl."

This appeared to be a more difficult question. The old man studied the picture carefully. Adrienne stopped breathing. Finally he smiled with wrinkles at the sides of his eyes, and he answered in a clear, clipped language that sounded to her vaguely, hauntingly familiar.

"Samuel saw a child only for a moment, and he can't be certain it was the child in these pictures. He says he knows only that the girl had very light hair, like this child, and she was about this age."

Adrienne studied the dark eyes that seemed to look right through her. The description was close enough! She must have been the child the old man saw! Blond two-year-olds weren't plentiful in Julius Bay. "Were there any white people living in the village at that time?"

When the interpreter repeated her question, Samuel shook his head.

"What about the surrounding area? Were there white people near? Farmers?"

An exchange of words. "These are tribal home-lands," the Indian answered. "Mostly only Xhosa peoples live here. The great region of hills to the north, the Transkei, is populated by Bantu tribes, no Europeans."

The old man had stopped smiling. He was gazing at the two photographs of Adrienne at the age of two, photos taken, according to her mother, at the time of her arrival in Boston. In a soft, clear voice, Samuel murmured something while he scratched his head and looked up once or twice at gathering clouds in the dusky sky.

The Indian looked at Samuel strangely, then proceeded to translate his words for Adrienne. "Samuel says there are stories about a European child living in one of the African hamlets about a quarter century ago. The people believed the baby came out of the ocean...sent as an offering from sea spirits."

Adrienne sucked in her breath. "A white child living with an African tribe?"

Samuel was continuing in a droning voice. The hotel man translated. "The baby disappeared from the hamlet. Some say the sea spirits came and took it back. Others say it was carried off by hyenas. And still others believe it was taken away by government officials from Pretoria."

Adrienne stared at the two men in stunned silence. Her lips were trembling.

The Indian smiled. "It's only a story, madam. A fable. There are many fables among these people."

Only a fable, the logical half of her brain echoed. And yet a child was here—*she* was here, with her mother. And she had to have come from somewhere. "Are there many native villages near Julius Bay?"

"Not many close by. They are scattered about the hills."

"I'd like to visit some. Would it be possible for me to hire a car with a driver who knows this area?"

She saw surprise mix with suspicion in the Indian's eyes. "Yes, I can employ you a car and driver. Has this something to do with your mother?"

"With Samuel's fable. I want to try to find out if the story is true."

"Perhaps no one knows."

"But perhaps someone does know," Adrienne said, forcing a small smile. Samuel was looking at her so intensely she felt he knew more English than he pretended, and probably more of the reason for her quest than he pretended.

And the quest seemed suddenly enormous and impossible, like chasing a falling star. Adrienne realized with a heady snap that she was overcome by exhaustion. The jet to Johannesburg, then to Port Elizabeth, and the shuttle flight to a rural airport some thirty miles from Julius Bay had been long and exhausting. Brief naps on planes hadn't provided rest enough to steel her for a story like the one she had just heard. Her body had gone weak and shaky.

"Tell the driver I'll be ready any time after ten o'clock in the morning," she said while she zipped the photos into her shoulder bag. She wanted out of the early-night chill, away from the strange smells of the hotel kitchen, which were seeping into the back garden from an open window. Just a bed was all she wanted—her bed in the room with a view of the ocean—the one the proprietor said was the largest and best room he had. It may have been the very room she and her mother had shared one long-ago night before they'd traveled to Boston together to the big brick house that was to be their home.

An hour later she stood at the window of an almost-dark hotel room, wearing a pale-pink satin robe, looking out at the ocean beyond the little roofs of the village. Thoughts of Ken floated and darted through her mind—thoughts of his confusion over her mysterious flight from him. And the incredible story of a nameless child was disturbing and wouldn't leave her. In the day's last light she could see outlines of little fishing boats along the shore. The village below was quiet, but for voices near the shops and the barking of a dog, and the distant, whispering sound of the Indian Ocean.

A chill came over her. Shaking, rubbing her arms, she staggered backward to the bed and sat down, her chest tightening. "My God!" she muttered aloud. "If my name really means 'woman of the sea,' as Aunt Hester said, why would mother choose it and insist on it?"

Adrienne trembled with fatigue, tightly strung emotions and a nebulous fear. She realized now she was a fool to have come here alone. In this remote spot on the fringes of civilization, she had never felt so lost or so lonely in her life.

KEN HAD WALKED ADRIENNE TO HER CAR when she'd left the lab. The earlier warm promise of passion had been spoiled that morning by their argument. Everything was spoiled. He had felt her tense emotions, her disappointment, matching his own. Disappointment not just for that morning's unquenched thirst, but for tomorrow's, too. For how many unshared tomorrows? Were they countable? Were they forever?

In a hollow voice, he had asked, "You really don't know if you'll come back to San Diego?"

Her eyes had projected the same glimmer of fear he had seen the first time she'd spoken of Africa. "I'm...just not sure."

"Adrienne..." He had tried to capture those evasive blue eyes. "Is there something wrong? Something about this sudden decision—"

"No," she had interrupted weakly. "No, it had nothing to do with you—really. I wouldn't have left...this soon, but..." Her words were choked off by emotion.

"Are you sure you're okay?"

"I'm sure."

"Will you let me know what your plans are?"

"Yes. Of course I will." She had stood on her toes to kiss his cheek, then ducked hurriedly into her car, afraid to linger another second, he knew, to avoid both his questions and her own tears.

She waved once as she drove away. He had waved back, but he was frowning.

An hour later he was sitting at the word processor in his office, transferring notes of the past two days to permanent records, while he fidgeted, unable to concentrate. Slamming papers around the desk didn't help; neither did kicking a wastepaper basket halfway across the room.

Melanie Stevens, who sat on the other side of the office, typing, looked up from her work. "If you keep throwing things, I'm going to have to wear a hard hat. It's dangerous to be in here with you!"

"It looks like what he's throwing," Brian said from the doorway, "is a tantrum. What the hell's the matter with you, Ken?"

His answer was a scowl, followed several ripe seconds later by a stream of complaints. "I'm sick of trying to do everything with my left hand! This cast is driving me nuts!"

"Where's Adrienne?"

"On her way to Africa."

"Does that mean she'll be late getting here this morning?"

Ken slammed a notebook against the desk. "Why do you always have to play the clown, Brian?"

"You mean she really is leaving town?"

"Leaving the country. The continent!"

"Why?"

"How should I know?"

Feeling Melanie's eyes on him and pressure from Brian's interrogation, Ken pushed back his chair, turned off the computer and stomped out of the room.

His best friend was right behind him. Brian caught up as Ken started across the lawn. "You jerk, Ken! You let her get away?"

"I didn't let her do anything. Adrienne's a free spirit. She does what she wants."

"And she wanted to leave, huh?"

Ken glanced helplessly at the sky, shining bright blue between the branches of the trees. "Whether she wanted to or not, she did."

"Why did she pick Africa?"

"She didn't tell me why. Maybe she's inherited six or eight diamond mines!"

"Did she go alone?"

"I don't know."

"You sure don't know much."

"No, dammit! I sure don't."

Brian lowered his voice and his eyes. "You two were getting along so well. I was hoping this attraction could lead to great things."

"We had that discussion a long time ago, Brian. And I told you then to forget it."

"I'm thinking about the lab! About survival!"

"And I'm thinking of Adrienne!"

Brian glanced at him sideways, a look combining shock and disgust. "Yeah? Then something's changed. The last time I brought this up, it was you you were thinking about."

Ken picked up his pace, but the older man, half jogging, was keeping up with him.

"Listen, Brian...she was born an aristocrat. She's always had the best in life. She always will have."

"What's the best? Emeralds and caviar?"

"I don't want to talk about it anymore!"

"Okay! All right! Where the hell are you going in such a hurry?"

Ken gave him no answer; he didn't know the answer himself.

"If you're not going to finish transcribing that stuff, I'll have to do it, or we'll be too far behind schedule."

"Will you take over? I have to leave off for a little while."

"Well, calm yourself down before you come back to the office, will you? Melanie is high-strung enough without your tantrums influencing her."

Minutes of that morning crippled by. Ken sat at the pool edge, shading his eyes from the eastern sun, watching the dolphins, who clicked and beeped a language he could not understand. Ulysses seemed restless. Ken thought of how the big dolphin had actually tossed the ring to Adrienne when Aphrodite couldn't get the computer message. Unbelievable—yet he'd seen it himself. Adrienne's rapport with dolphins surpassed anything he had experienced in his years of working with them. Maybe she really did care about them as much as she claimed. Still, how could she have such feelings, considering her life-style and her background. Her world was saturated by human wealth, materialistic human values.

Ken had to grit his teeth with the realization that he had driven Adrienne away, pulling her to him one moment, pushing her away the next. But why Africa? Africa haunted him; he couldn't shake the nagging feeling that something was wrong. The trip had come up too suddenly. Maybe Adrienne was in some kind of trouble and she was alone.

He picked up a rubber ring from the edge of the pool and tossed it across the water with fury. Ulysses raised his enormous head and beeped out a Delphic scolding, sliding back and forth in the water. "What's the matter with you now?" Ken yelled at him.

The dolphin dived swiftly, then surfaced with the ring on his snout. He made a small leap and tossed the ring back to the man, still beeping and squawking. If Ken had had two arms, he might have caught the ring, but it sailed past his head and thumped on the cement, bouncing on its side. The man stared back at the eyes of the dolphin. "I don't believe this! After all these months, you pick now to decide to talk to me?"

Sensing all this had something to do with Adrienne, Ken struggled to his feet, kicked the ring—and regretted the impulse with the aching sting of his bare toes. He turned and sulked back to his small apartment to look for his shoes.

ROCK MUSIC WAS PLAYING LOUDLY in the background as Carmen opened the door. "Kendall Burke—of all people in the world! Since you phoned, I've been pacing in tight circles. You said you wanted to tell me something about Adrienne."

"No, I wanted to ask about her."

"Oh. She told you she was heading for the Dark Continent?"

"Yeah, she told me. But she didn't say why."

"Well, that doesn't surprise me. Come on in. I know it's still early in the day, but let's have a drink."

"Thanks. Why not?" He followed her into the bright living room, relieved when she turned off the stereo.

"I've been perfecting the margarita. Nine margaritas out of every ten made by bartenders are inferior to mine. I'm trying to make it ten out of ten. You can be a judge."

He stood fidgeting at her kitchen counter, courteously trying to hide his impatience while watching

Adrienne's perky, dark-haired cousin bustle around her kitchen in shorts and a long, loose T-shirt. He waited while the blender screamed and she served up a frothy drink, then led him back to the living room.

Carmen curled on a chair like a cat, her bare feet under her, facing him. "Well, what's your verdict, Ken?"

"Ten out of ten," he said with a smile, wiping salt and froth from his lips.

She grinned and set down her glass. "I can tell you why Adrienne left, but I don't think she'd want me to."

"Why not? Has she gone off to marry an African chief or something? Or did she just want to get as far away from me as possible?"

"Is that what you think? Adrienne's in love with you, you idiot."

He glanced away self-consciously, toward the palm branches moving lazily outside the window. "She was afraid of something, Carmen. I admit I'm generally an insensitive clod, but I couldn't miss the fact that she was scared."

"That's why you came? You thought she was scared?"

"Yes. I want to know what's going on. I thought I'd have trouble breaking through your loyalty to her unless I made my plea in person. I want to know if she's traveling all that way alone, and if so, why."

"Yeah, she's alone, which is really dumb. She wouldn't listen to me."

Ken sat forward and searched her dark eyes. "I'm here because I care, Carmen. I only wish Adrienne realized that."

Carmen gulped her margarita, then set it down, licking her lips and studying Kendall Burke's worried blue eyes. "It's no big, grand secret," she began cautiously. "It's just something Adrienne is sensitive about. She's on her way to some remote African village looking for her roots. Isn't that the kick of kicks?"

Stunned, he sat in mute silence while he listened to Carmen Janssen's account of Adrienne's personal struggle with an unknown past. By the time she had finished, his margarita glass was empty and his earlier anger had turned to taut anxiety. "I don't understand why she didn't tell me."

"She's afraid of what she'll find, I think."

"What could she possibly find?" Ken was leaning forward in his chair.

"I can't imagine. Maybe nothing at all."

"If she doesn't, that will tear her up, too. She'll be at a dead end."

Carmen sighed deeply, uncurling her legs from under her. "My cousin isn't as fragile as she looks. Since I've got to know her these past weeks, I realize she's one of the strongest women I've ever met. She's bounced back from some terrific blows. First her mother's death and then the breakup with her fiancé, which, incidentally, was over this inheritance thing. Richie Rich didn't want to get stuck with a pauper. Boy, did his white stripe seep through his perfect, custom-tailored exterior!"

"Could she lose her inheritance?"

"I don't know. Adrienne hasn't shown much interest so far in fighting over the money. She's too concerned with finding the secret her mother was guarding all those years. She wants to know who she is."

Carmen rose from the chair and picked up an open Atlas from the table. She laid the book over his lap, pointing with a long red nail. "Look at this place, Ken.

Right here at the bottom of the African continent. Can you imagine any place more remote? How could someone who looks like Adrienne come from a place like this?"

He got up suddenly, impatiently, thanked her for the drink and the information, and left her apartment with his head whirling.

From Pacific Beach he turned toward the marina, driving slowly, lost in thoughts and regrets. As he neared Shelter Island, his speed increased measurably, even recklessly. He sprinted down the pier. Once on the deck of the *Firefly*, he had to unbutton his jeans to get the keys from his pocket.

Inside, he was faced with the presence of Adrienne, still there, like a sweet apparition. The bunk, unmade since last Monday, was still rumpled from their love-making. Her towel lay crumpled on the floor where he had thrown it. Her lipstick was on the dresser top. The musty, closed cabin rocked gently with echoes of her laughter.

He slammed about the boat like a caged animal, before he plopped onto a bench in the main cabin and picked up the phone.

11

WIND WHIPPED at the wood-framed windows of Adrienne's second-story room. A morning rain blew against the glass, tapping a thin, dismal song. She awoke slowly, fighting back the urge of sleep that bade her stay a little longer in its protective refuge. Lying still, listening to the lonely sound of the rain, she felt empty and lost. In the cold light of morning, the superstitious legend of the child of a sea spirit had no more substance than a dream. It would dissolve into vapor if she got too close—a mere illusion, eerie coincidence. Just a tribal folk tale.

Desperation more than anticipation had motivated her to hire the car. She had to do something, even though she had nothing but a wild story to act on. And yet, as a fluttery weakness engulfed her again, she could not ignore the name her mother had chosen for her: "woman of the sea."

The hired driver didn't arrive until after twelve o'clock because of mechanical problems with the car. By then the rain had stopped. The air in the village, washed clean, was fresh and free of dust.

Wearing tan slacks, a white silk blouse and a tan sweater, her leather handbag tucked under her arm, Adrienne met the driver on the hotel porch. Uncertain about how she was going to explain her strange mission to the guide, she wondered if his knowledge of English would be adequate to understand.

As it turned out, the driver, Joseph—a tall, slim young man with pleasing, even features and very black skin—spoke English well. He told her the hotel proprietor had made it clear the American woman wanted to tour the countryside and visit some of the hamlets, but he hadn't said why. Joseph assumed she would be taking photographs, and he lamented their misfortune in choosing such a cloudy day. Opening the car door for her, he explained hurriedly and proudly that he had grown up in the hills north of Julius Bay and knew the country well. If he noticed his passenger was not carrying a camera, he made no mention of it.

She waited until they were underway to begin her barrage of questions about the legend of a white child who had once lived in a native village. Joseph told her he had heard the tale when he was a boy. The child was female, he said, with long hair made of seaweed, and some claimed she was actually a mermaid. The sea spirits left her on the beach one day, either accidentally or on purpose. There was much disagreement about whether she was left there as a gift or whether the spirits meant to reclaim her after a time. The child was running along the shore one day, when the sea took her back and no one ever saw her again.

Joseph did not know which hamlet, or kraal, might have originated the story. But he would ask, he promised, during their tour, if she was interested.

The day was dismally bleak. Wind blew from the south, gusting and chilly—a day to match Adrienne's mood as it became increasingly clear how hopeless her mission really was. They stopped four different times in rain-soaked little villages, some of which were no more than a few thatched-roof rondovals clustered together. There were sheep grazing the hillsides, and crudely built pens for the animals near each of the kraals. Joseph would park a fair distance from the huts, and Adrienne, feeling the discomfort of an outsider, would wait by the car or inside the car, when it was raining. She felt the age of the culture and of the land: thick, unbounded coils of hills, windblown grasses, round, sharp-roofed huts against a white-gray sky, silhouettes of dark, human forms moving about, some carrying large bundles of sticks on their heads.

Joseph was able to learn nothing more than he knew already about the myth, except that many people held the belief that the story was true. What fortified Adrienne was old Samuel's claim that he had actually seen a little girl. She believed Samuel, because he had been right about her mother's previous visit and about the DuVeaux sisters.

By late afternoon, the sporadic drizzle had turned to hard rain. Road tracks began to fill with water. Discouraged, they headed back to Julius Bay.

Adrienne said, "Since the stories about the white child all have to do with the ocean, maybe we should concentrate on the hamlets nearest the coast."

"I have similar thoughts," Joseph replied, squeezing the steering wheel with both hands as he guided the small car over bumpy, rain-sogged roads. "We can go again tomorrow, if madam wishes."

"Yes, I want to go tomorrow."

He flashed a toothy smile. "Such a tour is unusual, madam. Visitors seldom stay at Julius Bay more than one night. Photographers sometimes visit the Wild

Coast, and fishermen come." He switched on the car lights. The windshield wipers swooshed in steady rhythm—tinny, squeaking scrapes along the glass. He squinted through the slashing rain. "Details of these old local tales get all mixed together over the years. Maybe no one knows the truth anymore."

"Yes, I'm sure that's true. Nevertheless we'll give it another try, if you are willing. I've come too far to give up before exhausting all possibilities."

The rain fell like needles of loneliness. As she sat in the old car, jouncing over an unfamiliar landscape, Adrienne felt the loneliness. Her mind replayed the day she had visited Ken at the marina. It had been raining then, too, on that day so far away. Ken had seemed so vulnerable in one way and so puzzlingly aloof in another. He had been such an enigma then.

The mystery surrounding Kendall Burke had dissolved as she had come to know him, because of his frosty honesty. There was no mystery in his defiant stand against commitment to her; his life and his heart were already taken. The irony of it was that she could so easily understand the addictive lure of his life's work. With dolphins, he lived in a circle of so much love and awe. Ken evidently doubted there could ever be enough left for her. Still, Adrienne thought with a lump of sadness welling up in her throat, how could there be boundaries and limits on love? Life could stretch to the very edges of the universe with love's vibrations! Loving one could not make a person love another less! No, it was something else with Ken. Responsibility was what he didn't want. Emotionally, he had no room for sharing in his world.

Adrienne realized vaguely that Joseph had been telling her about the years he had lived in Port Elizabeth since leaving the homelands on his seventeenth birthday. His story had probably been interesting; she wished she had heard it.

They returned to the hotel in twilight. Without enthusiasm for anything but a hot meal, Adrienne chose a gray wool skirt and sweater and didn't bother with any makeup except for a brush of lipstick.

A simple change from pink to crisp white tablecloths, with red candles for each table, had converted the tearoom to a dining room. A fire was blazing in the stone fireplace. Only three tables had been prepared for the evening meal and one of the three was still empty. The second was occupied by two men, who initiated jovial conversation with Adrienne the moment she entered the room. They introduced themselves in strong Scottish accents and talked about their sports-fishing expeditions along the Wild Coast. Afterward they joined her at her table for a brandy.

She was glad for their company and for their laughter; it took the edge off her loneliness. After today's hours with Joseph—dark, rainy hours spent in the shadows of some fragile, moss-grown fable—she was beginning to fear finding the answer to her mother's visit here as much as she feared not finding the answer.

Emotionally drained, she excused herself after an hour of conversation and went upstairs to her room to read in bed until sleep could overtake her. The room was cold. Rain continued to pelt the windowpanes. Wind drowned out the sounds of the village and of the sea. Dread of tomorrow, of all tomorrows, came sliding down over her like a veil of darkness. And sleep, when it finally came, was fitful and full of pagan, otherworldly dreams.

In the night, the sound of knocking woke her. Frightened, she lay very still, shackled by the darkness, and listened. The rain had stopped; the wind was blowing more gently now against the window.

The knocking again! She sat up, turned on the lamp beside the bed and squinted at her watch. Three-fifteen in the morning! Who could be outside her door at this hour?

The knocking came louder. She drew up her knees, trembling, when she heard someone trying the lock! Frantically wishing there were a phone in the room, she rose from the bed and padded noiselessly across the room, and pressed her ear against the door to listen. She jumped, startled, when the knock slammed loudly just at the level of her ear.

The chain lock was secure. With grim caution, she unlocked the door and cracked it open just enough to peek out with one eye.

"Adrienne! It's me."

12

"KEN!" This was a cruel trick of a still-dreaming mind. It couldn't be Ken out there! She yanked at the door with frenzied ebullience, only to have it catch with a shivery bang against the taut chain lock.

"What do you mean, you might not come back? That's a hell of a thing to say to me, Adrienne!"

She flung open the door. "Ken! How can it be you?"

"It's only what's left of me after that nightmare of a trip. Why couldn't you have flown off to someplace simple, like Kansas City?"

Adrienne searched her spinning mind for words she couldn't find, while the living ghost before her smiled, set down his small suitcase and bent to kiss her. In the wondrous, unplanned joy of reunion, his kiss held less passion than love.

"Aren't you going to say hi?"

"'Hi' was my next line." Her voice was as dazed as her eyes.

His lips pressed to hers again, gently. "Why didn't you tell me the reason you were coming down to the bottom of the planet Earth?"

"You were so determined to think of me as pedigreed, I didn't think you could take the shock."

"I hope the real reason makes more sense than what you just said."

She flushed. "I was just...scared, I guess."

"That's what I thought. When Carmen weakened under relentless pressure and told me where you were and why, I got worried. I didn't like the idea of your pursuing this ghost hunt alone."

She stared, still unable to absorb the shock of his sudden appearance out of a stormy night. "You were worried, so you followed me halfway around the world? I don't believe this!"

"Neither do I. But I thought, a girl traveling alone, and without her lipstick..." From his coat pocket he took out a gold tube. "You left it on my boat."

"Now try me with the real reason."

He kissed her hand. "I'm not a patient guy, Adrienne. Not knowing when you were coming back—or even if you were coming back—was just too much for me."

She searched his blue eyes, gratefully questioning his decision. His clothes were rumpled and damp from rain, his hair uncombed, and a blue shadow of beard darkened his face. "You look exhausted."

"Ready to drop. Can I drop on that bed?"

"You can do anything you like on that bed."

"Lady, I'm going to remember you said that." He sat down on the bed and kicked off his shoes. She helped him with his damp jacket, still believing that at any moment she would wake to lonely, blowing rain in a stark, cold room to find she had dreamed him.

Ken was studying her carefully. "Are you okay, Adrienne?"

"Yes, I'm okay." *No, I'm really not okay. I'm crazy in love,* her heart was whispering with every beat.

He nodded his relief, yawned deeply and touched her pink gown. "You really do sleep in satin!" Another yawn, for which he apologized. "I've been two days without sleep and so wired with anxiety, that now, the minute I reach you and relax for a second, I've become a limp rag."

"You need to sleep. We can talk when you wake up."

"What have you learned? Do you know why your mother came to this...town or whatever this is?"

"I've found nothing concrete. Just a rainbow to chase, which is so crazy you couldn't absorb it in your present state of fatigue."

"I could try."

She smiled and kissed his forehead, brushing back his dark hair lovingly. "Morning is soon enough." Impulsively she threw her arms around him. "Ken, I'm so glad to see you! I was feeling so alone and frustrated, and not half as courageous as I thought I was. I still don't quite understand why you decided to come all this way, but I'm so glad you did!"

"I figure there is at least one time in everybody's life when he or she needs a friend standing by. And I want to be that friend for you."

"But this is far beyond the call of friendship."

"Makes one think we have a pretty special friendship, doesn't it?" he said with a smile, flopping over backward onto the bed.

"Let me help you," Adrienne offered, urging his legs onto the bed with the rest of him. She pulled off his socks and unbuckled the belt of his tan slacks.

"I'll undress you and tuck you into bed, and then I'll tuck myself into bed beside you. To keep you warm."

"Who said there isn't a pot of gold at the end of a rainbow?"

She had loosened his pants. "And who said he never wears underwear?"

"'Never' doesn't include traveling."

"Do you travel enough to have an up-to-date passport in the drawer with your emergency underpants?"

"I told you, I go to Australia every few months."

While she was unbuttoning his shirt, he lay still, his eyes closed. He raised himself zombielike to help her get the shirt out from under him, then lifted his hips so she could slide off his slacks. When he lay in only a pair of briefs, Adrienne called on all the combined powers of the ancient gods to resist touching him, to be fair and reasonable about his state of fatigue. But her fingers fairly burned to touch him.

She started to lift the blanket over him, when he opened his eyes and mumbled, "I always sleep nude."

"Of course you do. How could I forget?"

When he lay naked, she gazed down at him, feeling the fluttery whirls of arousal within her. "Hmm. One might suspect you're not as tired as you think."

"Your undressing me would have this effect, even if I were in a coma."

"'A coma'? Sure!" She took off her gown, turned out the lamp and slid into the bed beside him, snuggling against his hard, warm body. "Damn cast!" she muttered.

"In three or four more weeks I can hold you with two arms for a change."

Three or four more weeks, Adrienne thought with a twinge of panic. *I don't even know where, or who, I'll be then.*

He kissed her, his fingers in her hair, circling sensually at the back of her neck. Her heartbeat quickened with wanting him, but she knew this was not the right hour for making demands on him. Not even a man with Ken's remarkable stamina could withstand a trip from night into night, from summer into winter, without rest.

He whispered, "It's been a long time since I worried this much about someone. At least someone who isn't a creature of the sea."

"What if I were a creature of the sea?"

"Huh?"

"What if I didn't have any parents, after all, and instead I had come out of the ocean, like a dolphin?"

He smiled, stroking her thigh. "A mermaid? You don't feel like a mermaid. You're too soft, no scales. What are you talking about, Adrienne? You think you've reached a dead end?"

"I don't know. These are tribal homelands all around here. It's the most improbable place in the world for my mother to find me. All I have is a weird old fable, which I'll tell you about in the morning. You're almost asleep, poor baby."

"Almost. Not quite…" His fingers were caressing her abdomen now.

Adrienne rested her hand on his bare shoulder as he turned on his back, grunting with the weight of his cast. "It's so good to be close to you, Ken, when only minutes ago I believed you were so far away."

"Umm…yes, it's very good."

Sleep, my love, she told him silently as she lay in the dark beside him and listened to the comforting sound of his breathing. The wind was much calmer outside now, as if it, too, could settle down and rest. There was no sound of rain anymore. Down in the dark village she could hear a dog barking, and if she listened hard through the closed window, she could make out the constant washing of the ocean tides on the quiet shore. The songs of the night had changed. Even the ghost of her mysterious past, which stalked this sweep of the Wild Coast, did not move so ominously, now that she was no longer all alone.

Ken would understand. She should have realized sooner that he would never stand in judgment of her. He had come this far to tell her so, when she should have known it all along. She knew his values. He thought of her as a pampered rich kid with a privileged life. Yet it hadn't affected his feelings toward her. He had merely pointed out—too many times—their differences.

Her blood, whether blue or mongrel, didn't change the fact that she was Adrienne Canaday, heiress. There had been many Richards in her life; Richard Burroughs's attitude was so predominant in her social circles that she understood why her mother rarely discussed the fact of her adoption. Adrienne herself had put off telling Richard that her origins were questionable because she knew it would matter to him.

Ken was another breed of man. That the status symbols of the very rich meant nothing to him took some getting used to, as did the realization that whatever judgment he might ever pass on her would have nothing to do with the station of her birth. She should have given him credit for that.

Adrienne lay awake most of the night, caught in the fractured images of the kraals she had seen that afternoon and in the shock of Ken's unexpected arrival. Sleep refused to come with Ken's motionless body touching hers—or with anticipation of tomorrow balancing ominously on thoughts of just-still yesterday.

When the first yellow glow of morning sun began to show behind the thin white window curtains, the gently rhythmic sound of Ken's breathing lulled her into a doze.

She awoke to a heavy spray of light, a morning burning bright with sun. Yesterday's rain had gone. Ken lay asleep beside her, his bare chest moving evenly, his lips parted. She was staring dreamily at him, when his eyes fluttered open.

"Was I..." He cleared huskiness from his throat. "Was I snoring?"

"No. Do you snore?"

"I thought I might, sleeping on my back. Can't sleep on my stomach with this plaster in the way."

"Is that all you have to say this morning?"

He grinned sleepily. "I have a lot to say to you this morning."

"Aha! You must be rested."

"Rested enough." He grimaced. "But there's something important I have to ask you. Does this room have a bathroom?"

"Yes, through that door."

"Good. I hate streaking through cold hallways." He slid away from her and out of the bed, taking his warmth with him.

When he returned and stood for some moments above the bed, looking down at her, Adrienne found herself crazily wishing for a painting of Ken in the nude to hang in her bedroom, so in aged and graying years to come, night-borne images of this, the one true love affair of her life, could stay with her forever. When the world had all changed, this never would. In a bolted room of time, the picture of him as he was this moment would never have to leave her.

He drew the sheet from her naked body and studied her with pleasured eyes. "I could never tire of your beauty, Adrienne."

"I was thinking remarkably similar thoughts about you. Thoughts just as happy and just as sad."

"Why sad?"

"Because nothing is forever."

"My desire for you seems timeless." He dropped beside her, raining kisses on her, fresh and gentle kisses, over her face, her breasts.

"You're really here..." she whispered, responding to the newly familiar warmth of his lips.

"Let me prove I'm here."

A flush of heat warmed her stomach, her abdomen, her thighs—heat as his tongue was burning, sliding with new ease, pausing to inflict tiny lashes of fire where the sensation electrified her. She could hear gasps from her own throat filling the silent room as Ken's mounting passion brushed against the darkness of her doubts.

Richard had never done these things, not Richard or anyone. And yet with Ken it was so easy, so spontaneous, so smooth. The flowing together of bodies, emotions, needs, incautious possessing, was so harmonious, it was as if they were moved by music.

Ken's temporary disability required initiative on Adrienne's part, something he actively encouraged and that she enjoyed for both its freedom and its unique intimacy. Thus, instead of being a barrier between them, his broken arm in a way, brought them even closer.

Quivering emotions coiled in the heat of hottest summer, gradually unleashing themselves into a whirlpool of love. Quivering lips encountering undiscovered miracles of his manhood. Quivering thighs accepting the tense promise, accepting the width and depth of fulfillment.

So moments crashed upon one another vividly and wildly. And within the secret sanctuary of those moments were his eyes—asking, giving, loving. Losing all reality one moment, finding it the next and losing it again. Moaning, Ken rolled sideways, holding her, pressing deep and deeper. Her hands trembled through his hair, over his neck, across the prickly stiffness of his beard.

"Ken..."

"My love..." he breathed on an exhaling breath. "My only..." and the words gave way to accelerated breathing.

She embraced his rhythm, merging with him in symmetry of motion, losing herself to the chant of his moans. Even his fevered shudder, when it came, absorbed her completely, to become a part of her for those moments and forever.

IN THE QUIESCENCE OF AFTERGLOW, when the soft yellow light behind the curtains had become gold with the luster of an African morning, they lay luxuriating in the cottony fallen dust of passion.

Squeezing his hand, she asked, "Your only what?"

"Huh?"

"You were saying it to me, and then you couldn't talk anymore. You said I was your only something."

He squinted through half-closed eyes. "I can't remember saying anything. But I know you're my addiction. Besides cetaceans, maybe my only addiction."

"Go ahead and be practical if you want. You're much more romantic while you're making love to me."

"Stripped of my armor, you mean. With only my naked emotions showing."

"Yes, that's what I mean."

He smiled softly. "Your honesty is so refreshing."

"'Honesty'? I didn't tell you about my sordid past..."

"I don't mean that kind. I mean the important kind. You're very open about your feelings. I've tried to be, by telling you about my hang-ups and our..."

"I know—our differences!"

"Nothing can change those differences, Adrienne."

"Oh, hell! The big colossal difference you keep referring to is money, and we both know it. Didn't Carmen tell you I may not have any money? So now what will you use for a wall?"

"It's not just money. But let's not get into this again." Propped up on his good elbow, he never took his gaze from her eyes. "I want to know what you couldn't tell me last night because I was too tired to hear it."

Adrienne was jolted back to the present. The day was already upon her—another day of searching for something dreaded and unknown. Nevertheless, today would be easier, just because Ken was there, offering his strength for her to lean on.

"An old man who works at this hotel remembers my mother. He also remembers seeing a little blond girl. He told a story about a white child who is said to have once lived in one of the homeland villages. No one knows where she came from—the story is that she was brought by sea spirits—or what happened to her, except that she disappeared suddenly. I've been trying to find out if this child ever existed, or if the story is only a myth."

Ken lay in silence, looking up at the white ceiling. "What you're thinking is incomprehensible," he offered finally.

"I know that. But if the story has even one shred of truth, I have to pursue it, don't you see? I've learned I was here with my mother when I was two, just as the passports indicate. My mother came to Julius Bay twice. Would anyone come here a second time without a good reason? Ken, I know it's a crazy thing to do, but I'm trying to run down that story."

He rubbed his fingers thoughtfully over the sandpapery stubble on his chin; a puzzled frown furrowed his forehead. "Run it down how?"

"I've hired a driver to take me to the nearby villages, where he can ask the people what they remember about the story. Joseph is very clever and helpful, although yesterday yielded nothing but frustration. Useless as it may seem, we're going to try again to see if there is any possibility of finding the village where the myth originated."

"That's today's agenda?"

"That's it. Are you rested enough to join the expedition?"

"How soon do we start?"

"About half an hour ago."

"In that case, let's conserve time by sharing the shower."

She threw off the sheet hurriedly. "Only if you'll do it hot."

He grumbled, but he liked the heat just the same. In the shower, with the stream of hot water covering them and the little pit-pat of the spray hitting the protective plastic cover over Ken's cast, she soaped his back and made him squirm by taking liberties. He turned around and pulled her to him, kissing her while droplets of water sprayed their faces.

Pushing his wet hair back from his forehead, she smiled into his eyes. "I forgot to thank you for bringing my lipstick."

"THERE IS NO ROAD into the hamlet," Joseph told them as he brought the small car to a halt on the outskirts of a settlement only a short distance from a wide, white stretch of beach. "I have relatives here, so we will be welcome. I'm going to find my uncle. You can wait for me or come into the village, whatever you wish."

"Let's look around," Ken said, opening the car door to stretch his cramped legs.

She agreed. "No need to wait for us to catch up with you, Joseph. We'll just take our time."

The midafternoon sun, high in the sky, was beginning to move slowly westward. It was a warm day, with no signs remaining of yesterday's rain. Singing, Joseph sprinted down a well-worn path toward the hamlet, his bare feet kicking up small gusts of dust. His song faded on the gentle winter breeze as he disappeared.

Adrienne and Ken stood beside the car for several minutes, their hair blowing softly. They gazed south to where the ocean lapped the sandy beach, and north to grassy hills rolling out as far as they could see.

"It's beautiful," she said, shading her eyes. Heat from the bright African sun warmed through her yellow sweater and white wool slacks.

"Shall we head for town, milady?"

"I'm right beside you, sir." She took his hand.

The buildings were round, thatched-roof huts, larger at close range than they had appeared from a distance. There were crude sheep pens outside the cluster of huts. Although Joseph had disappeared from sight, they could follow his smudged footprints along the narrow path.

"I feel like an intruder," Adrienne said as they paused at the village edge.

"So do I. I don't see any welcoming committee."

The voices of romping children carried from the hillside just beyond. Goats and dogs roamed freely through the little settlement. Chickens wandered about, scratching in little patches of grass. A man wearing khaki shorts and a plain shirt came out of one of the huts, smiling in such a way that they knew he was already aware of their identity. He spoke to them in his own language, with the constant smile that translated as a welcome.

Three old women in colorful turbans were gathered at the open doorway of a rondoval, chatting while they stripped kernels from ears of maize with short-bladed knives. The women watched the strangers carefully, while a large black dog, lying in the sun beside them, twitched his ears and swished at flies with his long, crooked tail.

When the Americans strolled nearer the women, Adrienne's smile brought little response, save for the interest of the dog, who raised his head and blinked lazily. She reached down to pet the animal's big black head.

A sudden, unnatural silence fell. Adrienne sensed as much as heard it. Penetration of strange, black eyes. A bewildering hush. Something she didn't understand was transpiring.

She glanced at Ken. He was frowning. "What is it, Adrienne?"

"I don't know! Why is that woman staring at me like that?"

His arm folded about her waist protectively. "Maybe it has something to do with your petting the dog."

The eldest woman rose, saying something in her Bantu tongue that seemed to register astonishment. Puzzled, Adrienne faced the woman as the two others struggled from their sitting positions, whispering between them.

She felt Ken's arm tighten around her as they stood there, looking from one old woman to another, knowing something was wrong, helpless to ask. Slowly, fearfully, the eldest of the women reached for Adrienne's hand and took it in her own, staring for what seemed an eternity before she looked up into Adrienne's pale-blue eyes. It was a gentle, cautious touch, but firm. She drew nearer, gazing intensely, brushing fingers over Adrienne's hand.

"The scars! She's looking at my scars, Ken!" She felt her heart begin to thunder; her legs weakened.

More boldly now, the old woman touched the dark scars on Adrienne's left hand. Hushed voices gathered around them. The others were staring at Adrienne and coming near to gaze at her hand, but only the eldest woman had made any attempt to touch her.

"Where the hell is Joseph?" Ken muttered under his breath.

"He's coming," she answered with relief as she watched him move out from behind one of the huts in response to the commotion.

Before she had the chance to ask Joseph what was going on, the older women were gesturing and talking to him in whispered voices and pointing to Adrienne's left hand.

The mystified look on Joseph's young face as he turned to Adrienne caused another wave of fear to wash over her. It was a dizzy sort of fear, borne not on the threat of danger, but on the wings of a truth too awesome to comprehend.

"What are they saying, Joseph?" Ken asked.

"An incredible coincidence, very strange! They are saying madam is the child of the sea, come back again!"

Adrienne's voice came out in a high squeak. "This village? The child lived here?"

"Yes. The old women remember well. They see the scars on your hand and they look at you closely—your eyes, your face—and they remember." He squinted, half believing. "Can this be true, what they say?"

"It might be true, Joseph. I have reason to think I may have been that child. I wanted to visit the villages to see if I could find out for sure."

Ken moved his arm from her waist to her shoulder. "You have found out, love! They recognized those scars immediately. You couldn't ask for better proof. Incredible as it sounds, you've been in this village before!"

"It's beyond imagining." Adrienne breathed, looking at the dark faces surrounding her. Some of the dozen or so people appeared quite excited, while others kept a cautious, almost fearful distance. One thing was certain: the citizens of the tiny village were not treating her as a lost family member returning. They were afraid of her.

"The people believe the sea child drowned," Joseph said. "She belonged to the sea."

"Tell them I think I was taken from here by strangers." With shaking hands, she fumbled in her handbag. "Would you show them some photographs?"

Joseph's black eyes shone bright with fascination as he passed the two baby photos to the eldest members of the group. Here was a pretty two-year-old in a new white dress and patent-leather shoes, her white-blond hair newly trimmed and tied with a pink ribbon, surely far different from how she must have looked when they'd last seen her. Yet from the whispers, nods and stares, Adrienne knew what Joseph was about to say.

"It is the same child, madam. The baby who was here."

She closed here eyes, clutching the remaining photograph to her breast.

Ken asked gently, "Who's in the other picture, Adrienne? Your mother?"

"Yes. Oh, God, I'm afraid to ask! I'm so scared, Ken!"

He forced a small smile. "Anyone who could survive the shocks of the past five minutes can survive anything. Go ahead, show them the pictures."

Time stood still while she watched brightly turbaned heads tilting to get a look at the photograph as Joseph walked among the group. The sun was hot and glaring overhead. The air seemed close and stale with dust and the smell of animal pens. She leaned against Ken and prayed she wouldn't faint. His body felt solid against her—the only thing in the world that was solid at this moment in her life.

"This madam," Joseph said, handing back the picture of Laura Canaday, "came here once with other Europeans, taking pictures of the village and the people. One woman told me she saw this madam talking to the little girl."

"They're absolutely certain she was here? There's no mistake?"

"No mistake. No outsiders knew the baby was here before the European woman saw her in the village and talked to her."

Adrienne felt herself sag with the emotional overload. A story too incredible to be true was true! Her mother had found her, quite by accident, near a remote stretch of coast on the Indian Ocean. Adrienne had come from the tribal homelands of Africa!

The old woman who had touched Adrienne's hand stepped away to talk with Joseph, but Adrienne still felt the woman's eyes fixed on her. The eyes were soft and kind, and she ached to know what this woman remembered. This same woman might have held her once, or even sung her a lullaby. Sadness engulfed her. She wondered if the flight of childhood memory was a blessing or a tragedy.

Adrienne accepted the picture back from Joseph and tried to swallow, but her throat was too dry. Her voice was almost a whisper. "You say they believe the child drowned?"

Joseph's deep voice was edged with excitement. "They have been telling me the story. Everyone talking at once. I will translate. One day at dusk, when the tide was going out, three men were walking on the beach and found a baby sitting all alone by the ocean. She was wet and covered with sand, and she had very white skin and blue eyes and silver hair. When she saw the men, she was frightened and began to cry. They came near and she cried more, and they saw that her left hand was bleeding from a fresh wound, which they believed was a wound from shark's teeth.

"The people from the village arrived and saw that the baby had come from the sea with the high tide. They thought she was a gift to them from the ocean spirits because she was so beautiful. There had been an omen on the previous night—a strange light over the ocean, far away, like the setting of a tiny sun.

"Some say the baby was here half a year, but most say it was even less time. She often ran on the beach, and she would watch the tides for hours. The witch doctors said she wished to return to her ocean home. They believed the sea came one night and took her back."

"It sounds as though your mother went home just long enough to get forged documents, then returned and kidnapped you from the village. It must have been carefully planned, so carefully that I suspect she had inside help. Probably bribed someone." Ken's voice was so soft his words were barely audible.

"You're right. The facts fit together perfectly! Oh, Ken, I'm shaking so badly I'm not sure how much longer I can stand up. And the sun is really getting to me. I have to get out of here! This is just too much for me to assimilate!"

"It would be too much for anyone. Why don't we walk down along the beach?"

"Yes. . .the beach. Let's do." In a trance, she returned the photographs to her handbag. "Joseph, we're going to the beach. Perhaps we'll come back to the village again, but not today. We just want to be alone. We'll meet you back at the car later. I need some time to collect my thoughts."

Joseph smiled, gave a little salute and resumed animated Bantu dialogue with the men of the village.

"He's probably telling them you're an American," Ken said. "And theorizing about what your coming back here means. If they believed you were sent here by ocean gods, they may have almost worshipped you."

"None of this is familiar," she said as they walked hurriedly from the confines of the settlement center, out past the sheep pens, on a well-traveled, sandy path that led in the direction of the beach. "I'll take their word that I was here, but I remember absolutely nothing. Except. . ." She paused, wrinkling her nose.

"Except what?"

"Well, when I first saw those round huts yesterday with the pointed thatched roofs, I had a funny feeling I'd seen them before. And there was a certain smell in the village—sheep, maybe, or something the women were cooking, or a combination. I've smelled it before."

"You're still having a struggle believing it, aren't you?"

"Yes, even though I know it's true. No wonder mother never told anyone where I came from!"

Following the footpath, holding Ken's hand, Adrienne began to laugh. "Oh, Lord, what would Richard have done with this? My roots are in an African village. Oh my." She dissolved in laughter.

Minutes later they were walking the sandy white beach, hand in hand, listening to the waves sweep in at low tide and gazing out over a great expanse of blue to the horizon. A sea breeze teased their hair. A gull soared and dived overhead in the golden sea-fresh air. Years swelled in the lens of the sun. A beach unchanged.

Ken said, "Joseph described a light over the ocean. It sounded like a fire to me. A burning ship. Actually, the only place you could have come from was a ship, Adrienne."

"Yes, I know that. But it must have been awfully far out at sea if they didn't recognize it as a ship. I was just a baby, not even two years old. How in the world could I possibly..."

She turned to Ken. In the blinding glare of rugged winter sun, his eyes had lost their color and became as silver as the sea. Adrienne blinked wet, salty sunlight from her eyes. "The dolphins!"

She saw Ken swallow, saw his gaze pull away from the wild, heaving sea and return to her, the shine of tears in his eyes.

"My God, Adrienne! Now I understand! I understand everything!"

13

KEN SAT IN THE WINDOW SEAT of the jet liner staring out at a gray-white winter sky. Rays of morning sun frayed the edges of white clouds. The plane soared upward, leaving Port Elizabeth behind and below, leaving big ships swaying in the harbor, rising over the buildings of a rapidly shrinking city.

So began the second leg of their long journey home. By noon they would be at Jan Smuts Airport outside Johannesburg. By evening they would be above the Atlantic, flying west. Adrienne sat back in her seat, eyes closed, feeling the plane climb and listening to the sound of its engines.

Ken had been so quiet since the beach. He seemed as stunned over what they had found as she was. They had walked the beach in silence, hand in hand. Riding back to Julius Bay, they had barely heard what Joseph was chattering about in the driver's seat. Adrienne, too, had been very quiet since the beach.

Now Ken turned away from the window and touched her arm. "Have you thought over locating the ship's records to identify your family? It shouldn't be hard to do. There'll be records, Adrienne. We know where and approximately when that ship sank. I'm sure we can find out your real name, trace your relatives, before we leave South Africa."

"I have thought it over. The answer's still no. My parents surely died in the boat fire, Ken, and probably brothers and sisters, too, if I had any. I'm Laura Canaday's daughter. I don't want to be someone else."

"I don't quite understand," he said gently. "You came all this way to find out who you are."

"Yes, I thought that was why I came. Now I realize my motive was solely to find out why mother conspired to keep my identity a secret. It was the mystery I was trying to uncover, not my former identity. I know the secret now. And I know who I am. I'm the kid Laura Canaday traveled halfway around the world to snatch after she saw me running around a remote African village. Mother had to keep it a secret because she stole me!"

She smiled dreamily. "What a wonderful legacy, Ken! Laura knew the dolphins brought me from the sea. She had to know. And I think she intended to tell me someday. When I was little she loved telling me the story of Ulysses and the dolphins."

"Your mother could have checked ships' records to find your family name."

"She could have. But I don't think she did. As long as she didn't know where I really came from, she didn't have to quarrel with her conscience about stealing me and adopting me." Adrienne smiled sadly. "Don't you see, Ken? How it is with my mother and me? She didn't want me to be anyone but her daughter, and I feel the same now. I don't want to be anyone else, either. As long as I can remember I've always belonged to Laura, and I always will."

He met her eyes. "Forgive me for not being more understanding in San Diego, Adrienne. You asked me to believe how much the dolphins meant to you, and I refused to understand."

"How could you possibly understand? I didn't consciously know why myself."

There was a strange expression in Ken's blue eyes—sadness mixed with happiness. Adrienne wished she could read his mind. Her gaze dropped to her lap, and to the scars on her hand.

"Ken..." she mused after a long silence. "Joseph said some villagers believed my scars were the marks of shark's teeth. Do you think that's possible?"

He frowned. "No. I've seen and studied wounds from sharks' teeth. Those marks don't fit any of the patterns I've ever seen. And think how small a baby's hand is—sharks don't take little nibbles. But there are thousands of sharks in these waters, especially between Julius Bay and Durban. And you were bleeding, which would have attracted them. It's possible, even likely, that the dolphins who brought you to shore saved you from sharks, as well as from drowning."

"There was no sign of a lifeboat, according to the stories," Ken was saying. "And the ship was on fire. That makes me pretty sure there was an explosion aboard—no time for anyone to get off. It happens. And it would account for your injury. I'm only guessing, of course, but I'd say it's likely your hand was hurt before you fell into the water."

"You're awfully good at deductive reasoning."

"I've been around boats and oceans all my life."

"And dolphins."

"Yes. And dolphins."

She was pensive for a moment, thinking about the bond of kinship begun one faraway day in the open sea. "Why did they do it, Ken?"

"I can't answer that. Maybe someday we'll know. But hell, Adrienne, who can explain why humans do the things they do? I've heard some people theorize that dolphins may save people by sheer accident, that they're merely balancing an object, playing with it. But that's anthropomorphic ignorance. I believe the dolphins knew exactly what they were doing when they saved you. And they had their reasons."

She sighed and said carefully, "This discovery tends to dwarf our. . .our alleged differences somewhat, doesn't it?"

Ken became thoughtful. He blinked, and his eyes softened. "I'm sorry I made such a big deal about all that. I don't know what made me think money was so important." His voice trailed off into an uncomfortable silence.

"It would be a sad thing if money, or the lack of it, counted so much it could separate people who really love each other. . . ."

A flash of her last memory of Richard crossed her mind, with echoes of their conversation. It had certainly mattered more than anything else to poor Richard. This moment, though, on this plane, she hadn't meant to blurt out the word "love." Ken had never used that word. Through her wishful thinking, she had assumed too much. She felt foolish, and Ken's ignoring her remark only made it worse.

He merely smiled across at her with a sparkle in his eyes and asked, "Are you a millionaire, Adrienne?"

She forced herself to smile back. "My mother intended for me to be. Aunt Hester is determined I will be." Her eyes shifted to meet his. "Do you want me to be?"

"No."

"Uh-huh. You've made that pretty clear all along. Would it cost me your..." She sputtered and caught herself before she uttered that loaded word again.

He finished the question for her. "Would it cost you my love if you were? Of course not!"

Her eyes grew wide. "But..."

He reached for her hand. "I've been knuckling under to paranoia, or pride, or something. I tried to hide from my own insecurity by telling myself we didn't travel in the same circles or mingle with the same people, because of who you are and who I am. But I can't fool myself anymore. I know your values aren't much different from mine. Money wouldn't change those values one way or another."

Adrienne breathed a prayer of thanks inside herself. Finally he really did seem willing to tear down the wall he had always tried to keep between them. She swallowed and forced herself to pursue the subject of her inheritance. "Just before I left Carmen's apartment for the airport, Aunt Hester phoned to tell me she'd been in touch with my attorneys in Boston. Mother's will was under scrutiny by a judge and the attorneys weren't eager to quote their opinions as to what his decision would be. Said there were problems." She smiled at him once more. "I may be penniless. Would that please you?"

He looked very uncomfortable. "No."

"But I thought you said—"

"Dammit, Adrienne, I don't wish bad things for you! I don't want the money to matter at all! I don't even—" He looked directly at her eyes. "I don't even want to know!"

"Okay." She shrugged cheerfully. "When I find out, I won't laugh or cry. I'll be stoic and not tell you."

"You'll have to tell me."

"Why?"

"Because I'll...well, because I'll be there."

"Where?"

"Wherever you are."

Her heart began to hammer. "How can you be sure you'll be...wherever it is?"

"You said it was what you wanted, didn't you? Didn't you say you loved me, Adrienne?"

"You told me not to love you."

"I was an idiot. Do you love me enough to marry me?"

"To...to..." Her voice caught. Adrienne, in her shock, could only stammer, "To..."

He stopped her sputtering with a kiss, a soft, tender touch of his lips on hers. "I love you, Adrienne. I've loved you from the first day I saw you, and the harder I tried not to, the more in love I fell. I'm glad there's no decision about your inheritance yet. Now we can make our decision without that one getting in the way."

She was still struggling against the shock of Ken's words. "What...decision?"

"To get married. Do you think we should?"

Her arms encircled him, her head came to rest against his broad shoulder. "Yes! Oh, yes, I think we should!"

He hugged her tightly. "Could you adjust to my life-style? I'll get us a more comfortable boat...we could—"

Adrienne looked up at him, understanding why he had chosen now to ask her to marry him. Now, before he knew about the money. "Wherever you are..." she interrupted, echoing him, "is where I want to be...always."

KEN STOOD AT THE RAILING of the forty-eight-foot cruiser, *Dragonfly*, holding a coffee cup, watching a Florida sun rise over pleats of masts. From the cabin below, soft music rose to blend with the sounds of the marina, with echoes of human voices, with cries of gulls and with the smooth breathing of tides out beyond the water.

He finished his coffee and went below. At the piano, Adrienne jumped, startled, when she felt his arms come around her shoulder. She smiled as he leaned over to kiss her temple and squint at the scribbled, hand written music in front of her.

"The song is beautiful. What is it?"

"Something I composed for Ulysses, a sort of tribute. I miss him."

"I miss him, too, but the sight of him swimming away free, takes a lot of the sting out of having him gone."

"Do you think he'll be okay?"

"I hope so. We released him within a mile of the place he was captured and that group of dolphins seemed to accept him immediately as if they knew him."

"He'll have some interesting stories to tell them."

Ken laughed. "Yeah, I'd like to think so." He kissed her temple again, then her cheek. "I'd wanted to free him for so long, but the cost of flying him back to Florida was so prohibitive."

"You see, darling, money doesn't have to be a curse." She rose from the piano. "Does it?"

"I'll admit I wasn't sure at first. When the judge ruled that the legality of your adoption was irrelevant—that your mother's will would stand just as she wrote it—it was all so quick."

"It was the only just decision he could make, Ken. Mother didn't even know those other people."

"Well…" Ken said with a yawn. "That's all in the past and you're right, money doesn't have to be a curse."

The salon of the *Dragonfly* bore no resemblance to that of Ken's old *Firefly*. The spacious wood-paneled cabin, in which they had installed a custom-built piano, bespoke warm elegance. It was lit softly now by tropical morning sun.

Ken yawned again and stretched. "Maybe we should go back to bed. We fooled around too much last night and didn't get enough sleep."

"I thought you had a meeting with the ocean-musuem director this morning."

"I canceled. I've changed my mind about buying another dolphin. We can work with the ones we already have. So there's nothing more to keep us here. We can go home."

"It was freeing Ulysses that changed your mind, wasn't it? You've been thinking about the wild dolphins who swam up to him."

He nodded. "It isn't necessary to capture wild dolphins anymore. There are enough being bred in captivity for the research. Finally."

Adrienne curled up beside him on the cushions, brushing her fingers through his hair. "Oh, how I love you!"

He touched her face tenderly, gazing up into her light eyes. "You've made all the difference, my love. I thought my life had purpose before you came, but I was wrong. I was a loney man and didn't know it."

She smiled, showering him with little kisses.

He hugged her tightly. "Old Ulysses enlightened me the morning you left for Africa, when he threw his blue ring at me."

"Ulysses' ring," she mused. "Whoever would have thought that myth...?"

The boat rocked softly in the channel waters. Ken's fingers lovingly folded over her left hand, covering the scars of her past, touching the promise of their future—her wedding ring emblazoned with a bright, gold dolphin.

Surrounded by a cold and heaving ocean, the child clung desperately to a plank from the burning yacht. Bright spills of blood flowing from slashes on her little hand imbrued the silver water. In the pale pink glow of sunrise, approaching fins appeared as shadows on the restless surface of the sea.

As the rouge of morning sun brushed the water, crackling, sucking sounds came from the dying boat. The child panicked as the drifting plank began to slip away from her. Fins were now very close, very large, circling smoothly.

A large gray head broke through the ridge of swelling water. Dark and quivering, terror rose from the membranes of the sea, but was suddenly dispelled by one brilliant, gleaming eye—a strange and alien eye—that sparkled trust. A silky presence touched her tiny body underwater. Fear vanished in a light of silent communication beyond the child's life experience.

Gray forms swam under her, lifted her, held her at the surface. Tiny human hands grasped at a stiff dorsal fin, but were unable to hang on. The sea creatures buoyed the child, kept her afloat, and moved steadily away from the flames.

The baby felt the rocking of the open sea, the eternal, rhythmic breathing of the ocean. Sun and salt spray burned her light-blue eyes, so she closed them and, with the alien beings who held her, rode the swell of endless, dark-blue water.

She was not awake when they left her. But sometime later, when the light of day had turned to dusk, a small, white-blond head rose from a pillow of sun-warmed sand. Innocent blue eyes saw first the washing tides, saw foam bubbles hissing, popping on shining, pebbly sand. The child sat up slowly. Alone again, still wet, she shivered and began to cry.

Silhouettes of three human figures walking the beach formed in the distance. Figures of men with black skin, figures becoming larger, coming nearer.

Then there were more people, all with black skin and strange, mysterious voices. A woman with a soft voice and great black eyes knelt beside the terrified child and reached out to brush sand from pale little cheeks. Slender fingers lifted the bleeding hand and held it gently, as dark human forms drew around, chattering in hushed whispers. Discovery of the three deep, bleeding slashes on her own hand made the child sob harder.

The woman unwound a colored turban from her head and wrapped the tiny hand. Then she lifted the child, stroking the tangle of wet, white hair, and turned toward the land, toward the hills.

The child could see, as she was carried from the beach, the rising and dipping of fins out on the ocean surface. With a desperate cry, she stretched her baby arms to the creatures of the waterworld, not wanting them to leave her.

She fought for a bold future
until she could no longer
ignore the...

ECHO OF THUNDER

MAURA SEGER

Author of **Eye of the Storm**

ECHO OF THUNDER is the love story of James
Callahan and Alexis Brockton, who forge a union
that must withstand the pressures of their own
desires and the challenge of building a new television
empire.

Author Maura Seger's writing has been described by
Romantic Times as having a "superb blend of
historical perspective, exciting romance and a deep
and abiding passion for the human soul."

**Available at your favorite
retail outlet in SEPTEMBER.**

ECO-B-1

You're invited to accept 4 books and a surprise gift Free!

Acceptance Card

Mail to: **Harlequin Reader Service®**

In the U.S.
2504 West Southern Ave.
Tempe, AZ 85282

In Canada
P.O. Box 2800, Postal Station A
5170 Yonge Street
Willowdale, Ontario M2N 6J3

YES! Please send me 4 free Harlequin Temptation® novels and my free surprise gift. Then send me 4 brand new novels every month as they come off the presses. Bill me at the low price of $1.99 each ($1.95 in Canada)—a 13% saving off the retail price. There are no shipping, handling or other hidden costs. There is no minimum number of books I must purchase. I can always return a shipment and cancel at any time. Even if I never buy another book from Harlequin, the 4 free novels and the surprise gift are mine to keep forever.

142 BPX-BPGE

_____
Name   (PLEASE PRINT)

_____
Address   Apt. No.

_____
City   State/Prov.   Zip/Postal Code

This offer is limited to one order per household and not valid to present subscribers. Price is subject to change.

ACHT-SUB-1